The SOCCER diaries

The SOCCER diaries

BOOK 3
ROCKY GOES FOR GOAL
by Tom Palmer

REBELLiON

First published 2025 by Rebellion Publishing Ltd,
Riverside House, Osney Mead, Oxford, OX2 0ES, UK

ISBN: 978-1-83786-266-5

10 9 8 7 6 5 4 3 2 1

A CIP catalogue record for this book is available from the
British Library.

Designed & typeset by Rebellion Publishing
Cover art © V.V. Glass, 2024

Printed in Denmark

MIX
Paper | Supporting
responsible forestry
FSC® C104608

For my friend, Paul Hill.

Part One:
Quarter-Final

1

After training, Coach Abby asked Rocky to wait. Would Rocky walk with her back to the locker rooms? she asked. Just the two of them?

She had something she wanted to talk to Rocky about.

Rocky did as she was told, immediately noticing the eyes of her teammates and friends glancing back at her. What's going on? she wondered. Why are they watching me? Do they know something? Her next thought was bleaker. What have I done wrong? Am I going to be dropped?

But no. Rocky was pretty sure that was not going to happen. She knew she had trained as well as any other player, if not better. She always gave football one hundred per cent whether it was an important game, light training, or a kickabout with friends after class. Even so, her default reaction to anything different or the intervention of an authority figure—especially Abby—was to worry that something bad was going to happen.

"You know what I want to talk to you about, don't you?" Abby asked.

"You're sending me back to England?" Rocky half joked.

Abby smiled. It was a real smile. She often laughed at things Rocky said. Laughed like she meant it. And Rocky loved that she could do that with Abby: amuse her coach at the American school where she had a scholarship.

Amuse a coach who used to play for Team USA, had been part of World Cups, even had a winner's medal.

Now Abby's face became serious. "I want to ask you to be captain," she said after a pause. "For the finals. Of the state championship. We need a leader on the pitch. And, for me, that's you. If you can handle it?"

Rocky carried on walking step by step alongside Abby. She took a deep breath, preparing to answer.

Inside her head a voice was saying *Noooooooooo*. No, because she didn't want it to be her job to tell other people what to do. No, because she didn't want to have to lead by example in the middle of a match when the heat was on. No, because she had enough to process about her own game, let alone processing the games of her teammates.

But yes, because of who was asking. Abby.

And there was no one in the world she wanted to impress more than her coach.

"I'd be honoured," Rocky replied. "Thank you for asking me."

"Good," Coach Abby went on. "Now… your first job is to go into the locker room, take the room and tell your teammates. Can you do that?"

Nooooooooooo, the voice said again.

"Yes. That's fine," Rocky said as firmly as she could. "No problem, Coach."

They walked on. In silence. To the dressing room.

Rocky knew this moment was a test. To be captain, you had to be able to command the locker room, then command the pitch. You had to ask—even tell—people what to do. You had to lead. And look like you really expected people to listen to what you had to say, then for them to do it.

11

But this sort of thing? For her? For Rocky?

For days speculation had been rife about who would be chosen as captain.

Rocky was convinced it would be Kim, her best friend, the team's longest-serving player and wannabe USA international.

Kim had predicted it would be Naomi, the rock in their defence. A calm, strong, thoughtful presence on the pitch. Rocky had thought, in fact, that Naomi would be the best choice. Naomi was a born leader. Probably more suited to the role than Kim.

Naomi had said, all along, that the new captain would be Rocky. And she had been right.

Abby and Rocky continued to stride in silence towards the door of the sports changing rooms that the rest of the team had disappeared through moments before. Rocky stared at the school as they walked. At that huge glass façade reflecting the impressive sports fields, the row of trees, the range of hills beyond.

And her.

Rocky.

Yes, Rocky could see herself there, too. Her reflection walking towards the dressing room.

She saw that she looked tiny. She felt tiny.

What do I say? she asked herself.

"Hi everyone. Guess what…?"

Or.

"Surprise, girls… I'm your new leader."

Or.

"Sorry, Naomi. Sorry, Kim. I win."

Urgh. No. No. None of that. Nothing like that.

Through the door into the dressing room, Rocky felt sick now.

Be matter-of-fact, she said to herself. *Just*

tell them. Don't be funny or sorry or weak or strong. Just say it.

Into the dressing room now. Hit by the smell of sweat and the sour whiff from removed boots and shinpads. Disgusting. But comforting, too. She longed to sit down on a bench, peel her shinpads and boots off too, merge into the group, be one of the girls.

Was that over? That feeling? She wasn't feeling it now. And panic was starting to overwhelm her. Doubts and questions and fears rearing their heads. What did you do? How did you start?

And there it was. Already. It had happened already. She was no longer one of the girls, no longer part of the group. She was one step removed. Rocky felt it like an ache in her side even before she had told the others about it. And she felt like something had gone forever.

Rocky stood there, feet planted on the locker

room floor. She clapped her hands together twice, as loudly as she could. Doing exactly what Coach Abby did to get the team's attention.

A sudden silence. Now everyone was looking at her. The trick had worked.

"I've got a short announcement," Rocky said. Then that voice in her head again. *You don't want this.*

She had that idea in her head that she could just walk calmly to the door, open it, then run. Run and keep running. Away. A thought she had had throughout school. In classrooms and school halls back in England. In the hospital too, when her dad was dying. And at his funeral two years ago. The idea that— at any point in your life, however serious or important the things were that you were part of—you could just get up and run away.

That was how she felt when she opened her

mouth to speak. To say, "Abby's just told me that I am going to be captain for the next three games."

Make it about them, a voice came to her. *Not you. That's the way to play it.*

"I hope you'll trust me with this," Rocky carried on. "I am so proud to be captain of each of you. What you've achieved so far— what we've achieved—is amazing. I hope that I can help us all take this journey even further."

There. She'd done it.

Rocky watched nervously as her teammates stood and applauded, some cheering. Big smiles and whoops. Rocky felt a smile come to her face and it hurt. It actually hurt.

Now Naomi was on her feet, coming to shake her hand. Their hands clasped together, Rocky took a breath. "You're vice-captain, Naomi. Abby said I could choose a vice-captain. Will you accept?"

Naomi nodded. "I'd be honoured," she said, withdrawing her hand, but not touching her chest afterwards like she normally did.

Good. Naomi had been nice about it. That was good. Rocky needed to know that Naomi was on board. Naomi was Rocky's vice-captain. That meant that if Rocky was injured off or sent off, she would be the leader. They needed to be tight. They needed to be open with each other.

Didn't they?

Could they?

Rocky was torn. Because, deep down, she still thought Naomi would make the best captain, but she wasn't going to say that to Abby. You couldn't contradict Coach Abby. Abby was as close as you got to a football deity. She had a plan. And Rocky being captain was part of that plan. You wouldn't say no to a football god, would you?

Player after player shook Rocky's hand, following Naomi's example. It was a bit formal. Even a bit British, Rocky thought. But she was pleased that none of them hugged her. Though the last person to congratulate Rocky was Kim. And Kim did hug her. But that was okay. Rocky didn't want hugs... unless they were from her mum. Or from Kim.

Ten minutes after all the captain stuff was over, Rocky was the last to finish changing. She was pleased to have the showers to herself, had even taken it slow so that she could carve out time on her own. To think. She stood underneath the powerful spray of the shower head and let it hammer into her back and neck and then her face.

Captain.

She was captain.

Another notch. Another success in her

footballing journey. There was no denying that things were going well for her in the States. Being accepted on the scholarship at this school. Becoming one of the better players on the team. Being part of a team that had gone further than any team from Mountain Heights had gone before: the state championship. And now she was their leader.

Then—after all that progress—there was the other rumour too. The one about professional clubs from the US watching the Mountain Heights team to pick off any talented young players, whisk them away from the school and offer them contracts on a pathway to professional football. Did Rocky want that? For Kim? For one of the others? And, if she was one of the players chosen, did she want it? For herself?

Initially she'd not imagined it as an option. Then she could not believe it could happen to her. To someone like her. A girl from England. Just a normal girl. A nobody, really. Another body. Another football wannabe.

But now?

Now... she was considering it. Really considering it. Going pro was one of her options. The other option was staying on the scholarship and focusing on her education. An education that was going surprisingly well. For her.

Rocky stepped out of the shower and grabbed her towel.

She noticed her hands were trembling slightly and her heart was pounding in her throat. So much on her mind.

And that included the third option. To run. To run away from everything.

2

WHEN ROCKY WALKED into the apartment she shared with Kim, Naomi and Mahsa, she saw Kim sitting on the sofas at the centre of their sitting room. Kim was alone, water bottle in one hand, cell phone in the other.

"The other two studying?" Rocky asked.

Kim nodded.

This was normal now: Mahsa and Naomi shut up in one of their rooms, the soft sound of their voices testing each other on science and maths and literature. And as they did that, Kim and Rocky could be found watching YouTube on the TV, or chatting

21

over endless cups of hot chocolate or chai latte.

The quartet were definitely two twos now, rather than the group of four close friends they had been at the beginning of the school year. Things changed. Rocky knew that. Things always changed. But she had expected today to be a bit different. After the captain announcement.

Rocky glanced at Mahsa's bedroom door. "How were they?" she said in a quiet voice.

"About the captain thing?" Kim asked, leaning back.

"Yeah."

"Nothing said," Kim reported. "Nothing at all. But no weirdness. Nothing like that."

Rocky tried to smile. She was feeling anxious about Naomi and Mahsa now. Naomi in particular. "Right... so they just went in there and started working?"

"Yeah. Like we should," Kim said as she sat forward. "Shall we go into my room?" she asked, seeing Rocky look again at the other girl's door.

"Yeah," Rocky said.

Kim stood up and walked through her door. Past the large poster of the USA soccer team that Rocky's friend was fixed on playing for one day. Then inside the room, where a large tapestry of the moon and a wolf and symbols hung on the wall.

It was a nice room. Lovely, in fact. Kim had four plants on the window ledge that smelled gorgeous. And a huge plant in the corner that gave the room a completely different vibe. Like you were sitting outside or in a greenhouse in a park. There was a projector that cast rippling water on the ceiling some days, stars and comets on others. Kim had different slides she'd put in depending on what mood she was in, what she needed. Sometimes they lay together on their backs on Kim's bed and stared at the stars. Rocky loved those times.

Rocky loved Kim's style altogether. It made her feel calm.

Over Easter—while Kim's mum had been in hospital starting her chemotherapy treatment for breast cancer—Rocky had stayed with Kim at her beach house. The beach house was lovely and calm too, just like this. And posh. It was definitely posh. It overlooked a beach with views of the Pacific. The whole experience was amazing. Like being in one of those rom-coms set in California that she used to watch with her mum. With Jennifer Aniston or someone like that.

Either way, it was a world so nice and so different to what Rocky had known before.

It had taken her a while to get used to being

Kim's friend. Kim was rich. She had amazing houses—not just one house. And Rocky had recoiled from that at the beginning. She wasn't sure why. Part of her thought it was because she felt wealth was cheesy and she didn't want to be linked to posh people or people who had loads of money.

Another part of Rocky wondered if it was because she herself wasn't rich—not by British or American standards, anyway—and that something in her felt she didn't belong with rich people. That Kim or any of the girls at the school or in LA were too good for her, better than her. That they would think she was too poor or common or rough, or whatever words people in the USA used to describe poor or stupid or scruffy people like she felt she was.

Then Rocky found out that Kim's mum was being treated for cancer and all those silly barriers came down. And—as she came to know Kim better—she understood her dream, her drive, her obsession to play football for Team USA. Kim wanted to be the next Megan Rapinoe or Carli Lloyd. To achieve that, she would drop anything. She'd drop school. They all knew that she was driven to become a professional footballer, and to achieve that as early as possible. But how did you plan for something like that when your mum was having chemotherapy and you lived alone, your dad away on the other side of the continent in New York?

Even though it seemed an unlikely dream, because of her circumstances, Rocky immediately wanted to help Kim. To make sure she was okay, yes. But to fuel her ambition, too. So, after that, the posh house and wealth was nothing. Rocky had a friend who had a dream and—even though that dream might be to leave this school and take a pro contract—Rocky would do everything to help her make it happen.

What was that phrase? If you love someone, set them free?

That was it.

Rocky had never felt this before and it felt so counterintuitive to her, but she wanted Kim's dreams to come true so much she would even risk losing her as a best friend at school.

"Got to hand that poetry essay in on Monday," Kim added, continuing the conversation they'd had in the communal room and seeing Rocky glance at her laptop. "How far have you got with it?"

"I've done it," Rocky said.

"What?" Kim's mouth dropped open in shock.

"Done it."

Kim was laughing now.

Rocky got where Kim was coming from. She could hardly believe she was saying it herself. That she had done the poetry essay. That she had done it early. And something else… something she could hardly believe… that she was quite pleased with what she had written.

Rocky definitely was changing. She'd been nothing like this at school in England.

"The essay about the poem?" Kim asked. "Really?"

"Yeah."

Kim stared at Rocky, a massive grin on her face. Rocky could see her eyes were glistening. But she didn't comment on it.

They'd been asked to write a five-hundred-word reaction to a poem by an American poet called Sylvia Plath. It was called 'Crossing the Water'.

Reaction.

That was the word the literature teacher had used.

Reaction.

You had to react to it. Not critique. Not analyse. Not compare or contrast. Nor even explain it. Just react to it. So Rocky had reacted.

She had learned—from her mentor at the school, Jesse—that if you read a question properly you could save yourself a lot of time and confusion.

"What did you write?" Kim asked.

"I said I wished I'd read it two years ago," Rocky said.

"What? Is that it?"

"No. No, I put more." Rocky was quite excited to try to explain. The poem had made her feel funny, then sort of happy, she told Kim.

"Okay…" Kim said, still smiling.

"But that was the point of it," Rocky went on, eager to go into more detail. "I said that if I had read it two years ago, it would have made me feel better about something that happened in my life. You know. My dad dying. All that. I said it would have been good for me to have read it sooner."

"And did you say why?"

"A bit," Rocky said. "I mean, I went on about all the stuff in the poem about dark water and branches and how that reminded me of feeling sad. And that line where she says the leaves don't care. I loved that, so I put that, too."

"The leaves?"

"You know," Rocky said, astonishing herself that she was talking about poetry and actually being bothered about it. "When you get all sad and anxious and all that, it feels like your thoughts are everything. But, if the leaves don't care about what you care about, maybe it's not the end of the world. You know... the things making you feel bad. And... what did the teacher call it? An epiphany? When you realise something important? I had that. It was good."

There was a short silence. Kim had tears on her face.

Rocky still said nothing. She put her hand on her friend's arm, then passed her a tissue, trying not to think about the fact that, even though she had just been made captain for the finals and even though they were acknowledging she was doing so well at school, she felt tense. Really tense. Like her stomach muscles were being tied into a tight knot by invisible hands.

"You're doing so well," Kim said at last, wanting perhaps to mask the fact she had tears in her eyes, not wishing to talk about it.

"I thought you were going to get kicked out of school because of how you were doing, but now you're in the game."

Rocky knew that Kim was right.

When she'd come to Mountain Heights Rocky had got in because she had played pretty well at a summer school here. Really well, actually. But she didn't like to talk herself up, even inside her own head. She'd been offered a scholarship like Mahsa and Naomi. But that meant you had to do well in class, too. And Mahsa and Naomi were fine. Very studious. Amazing students. But school had never been one of Rocky's strengths and in the first term she had come really close to getting booted out because she was doing so badly. Then—with a bit of help from Jesse and her friends—she'd found a way of focusing in class.

And now this.

This!

This was the fact that Rocky liked doing most classes now. Liked learning. Even Maths and English. She needed extra help from Jesse and extra time in exams and all that, but that help was working. All that stress and tension and worry she had from school work was gone. Or at least diminished.

Rocky lay back on Kim's bed, facing her friend. And a question came into her mind.

So why—right now—do I still feel stressed and tense and worried?

It wasn't going away.

If school was okay, why did her arms feel like she was being stretched on a rack and her chest was being pressed down by a heavy weight? Along with her stomach muscles being knotted. And why had she felt like this all day?

She had only just realised that this was how

she had been feeling since breakfast. Even before she was asked to be captain.

There was sometimes a moment when Rocky felt so unsettled she had to stand up and try to fight this feeling physically. Or she'd go into panic mode. And she hated panic mode. Panic mode wasn't good.

So, Rocky stood up. She felt all crumpled up. Or crushed down. Or crinkled. Something. Maybe if Sylvia Plath, that poet, was here, she would have a better metaphor for how Rocky was feeling.

She knew what was happening now. Anxiety coming from within her like a sudden burst of lava from a volcano and her not knowing where it was coming from or why. Deep, deep down under the earth's crust.

Was it Kim being sad that was making her feel like this?

Was it her own sadness?

Was it that essay?

Or was it the football captain thing and the weird vibe at the end, and how Naomi and Mahsa had gone straight into their room after coming home and not stayed for a group chat?

Rocky laughed out loud. At herself. At the knots she was tying herself in.

She could try to attach her uneasy feelings to lots of things, but would she ever know if the feelings were caused by anything inside of her or outside of her?

Maybe she was anxious because she didn't know what she was anxious about.

Rocky laughed again.

"Why do you keep laughing?" Kim asked.

"I don't know. It's a funny mood day."

Kim nodded. "Yeah. I have them."

Rocky said, "I might go for a run."

"Again?" Kim sat up. "We only just finished training."

"I just feel… you know," Rocky said.

"Okay," Kim said. "I'll do my essay. You run. Then we'll go and have something to eat. Maybe off campus? Get away from here for a bit?"

"Yeah," Rocky said.

"The captain thing is big, Rocky. It'll take a bit of time to process."

"I'm not sure that's it."

"What?"

"Why I feel so restless."

"End of term coming?" Kim suggested. "That big choice you might have to make."

"Which one?"

"If you stay here at school or take a contract with a pro club."

"Me?" Rocky asked. "I don't think…"

"It'll happen," Kim said. "You're too good for it not to happen."

"To you."

"Or you."

Rocky shook her head. This was too much. The idea that she—or Kim—might suddenly not be here. Another idea to undo her. "I don't want to think about it," she said in a low voice.

A silence now. A slightly uneasy silence. Rocky rushed to fill it.

"But that's your dream," she said to her friend. "Going pro."

"It is," Kim conceded. "But it could equally happen to you."

Kim shrugged and Rocky thought again what that would mean. Kim leaving. Kim's dreaming coming true. Leaving Rocky on her own here at Mountain Heights. Did Rocky really want that?

She did for Kim.

"Sorry," Kim said. "I'm sorry. Go run. Forget I said it. Then we'll chill, yeah?"

Rocky nodded. She'd run. She'd think. They'd chill. But, while they were chilling, Rocky would be wondering why, whenever things were good and happy, she had to think about when and how that goodness and happiness would have to end.

Live in the moment, enjoy it for what it is. Was it her dad who used to say that? Someone had. But it was easier said than done.

As SHE RAN, skirting the woods on the edge of the school grounds and into the hills, away from everyone, Rocky thought about captaincy. She had watched enough games where the captain was vocal and it was obvious who was in command. And games where you didn't know the captain was the captain. Rocky always tried to work out who was a good captain and who was not.

Then her mind turned to Naomi and Mahsa's reaction to her being named as captain. The handshakes, the smiles. But Rocky knew that something wasn't right. She ran it through her mind. Naomi shaking her hand. But she had not, as she otherwise did, touched her hand to her chest after the handshake. That was what Naomi always did. It showed she meant the handshake sincerely. But she had not done it this time. And then her and Mahsa not being there when Rocky got back to their apartment. Did that mean anything?

Rocky was confused. She heard Abby's voice.

We need a leader on the pitch and that's you. If you can handle it?

Rocky had committed to that. To be the leader on the pitch. She could handle it. Yes, she could. On the pitch.

But what about off the pitch? What about now? Was she still captain in the corridors of the dorms?

Where was the line? Questions like that troubled Rocky.

So, she ran faster. Until it hurt. Until the pain in her lungs and legs was so much that she wasn't thinking about Naomi and Mahsa and Kim any more.

3

A FEW DAYS had passed at Mountain Heights.
Days of school work, football training and
chilling with Kim and some of her friends.

The day had been a good one for Rocky.
She'd slept well the night before and had felt
pretty good in all her classes. And, now, after
the last class of the day, Rocky went for her
weekly meeting with her school mentor, Jesse.

Jesse—as well as being a student mentor—
was Abby's assistant coach for the football
team. He was kind. He was calm. He was
supportive. And Rocky needed some support.
School was going fine. Football, too. But

during training, something had not been quite right. All along Rocky had been doing her best to be a strong captain with the other players. That was how she thought it should be. The style of being a leader. And most of her teammates had been fine with it.

Most.

But not all.

Rocky wanted to talk the whole captain thing through with Jesse before it festered in her mind. They met on benches outside the cafeteria. A coffee each—Rocky had recently got into coffee (with a flavour in)—they stared out at the open sports fields and the range of hills beyond.

Rocky loved those hills. They were where she ran when she was feeling anxious. And, when she couldn't run, she would stare at them and feel better. She loved hills. Hills were good.

But why? What was it about hills?

At home—in Melchester—there was a long range of hills. Long by British standards, anyway. They stretched up the middle of the north of England and were called the Pennines. Rocky could see them from her bedroom, from her school and from the Melchester Rovers stadium. They changed colour throughout the year, from pale, to green, to purple. And each day the light and the rain would change them, too. Sometimes snow would turn them white for a week or more. They were patterned with tiny dark lines, dry stone walls that had been built centuries before. Patches of heather. Squat trees that grew low because the wind would tear at them in storms.

When Rocky arrived in California, the hills to the north of the campus had lifted her, made her feel less worried that she was away from her town, her street, her house, her bedroom. Just to look at them boosted her. And made her want to go deep in among them, exploring, losing herself. She knew the hills well at home from walking and running and driving in them. She wanted to know the hills here, too.

"You looking at the hills again?" Jesse asked.

"Always," Rocky said.

Rocky knew this love for the hills had not gone unnoticed.

"And all set for the quarter-final tomorrow?" Jesse asked.

Rocky nodded, but said nothing. She knew that, if she thought about the game, she'd unleash the nerves and excitement that she'd need to draw on for energy tomorrow.

It was best to leave it leashed now.

"I read your essay," Jesse said, appearing to get where Rocky was coming from. "The one about the poem by Sylvia Plath. Thanks for copying me in."

"No problem. What did you think?"

"It was good," Jesse said.

"Thanks," Rocky said. And—once again—found herself eager to talk about poetry. Well, the poet anyway. "You know the poet. Sylvia. I mean… I know she was American, but she lived in the hills near where I'm from. In Yorkshire. She'd got hills, too. She's buried there. I looked it up. My mum and I are going to visit the grave when I go back in the summer."

"The poem affected you, then?"

"I suppose so."

"You went quite deep," Jesse said. "Did you want to talk about what you talked about? Or didn't talk about? In the essay, I mean."

"No." Rocky shook her head. "I don't need to."

Jesse laughed.

"What?" Rocky said.

"You're so direct. Are you all like that in Melchester?"

Rocky nodded, then frowned. She used to be proud of the idea that everyone where she came from was plain-speaking and direct. But it wasn't true. Not really.

"No," she said. "Actually, no. There are plenty of liars and two-faced people back home. Like everywhere." Then she asked Jesse, "Did you read the poem? 'Crossing the Water'."

"I did."

"And?"

"And what?"

"What did it do for you?"

Jesse seemed to squirm in his seat. "I don't... I feel... I never knew how to talk about poetry. But I loved your essay about it."

Rocky thought it was funny to find an adult who didn't feel comfortable talking about poetry. How good was it that she was putting him on the spot like teachers did to students, tricking you, trapping you, making you feel rubbish? And most of them weren't even doing it on purpose.

"You can hear Sylvia Plath read it on YouTube," Rocky told Jesse. "Try that. Don't read it off a page. I never do. I listen to stuff."

Jesse sat up straight. "You are doing so well, Rocky. Your teachers all say they're happy with you."

"Thanks." Rocky hid a frown.

So why am I feeling anxious still? she said to herself. Urgh, that question again. That feeling. She was sick of it, sick of herself.

Should she say so to Jesse? That was part of what he was there for, wasn't it? Her counsellor? Not just help with academic work, but what did they call it? Pastoral, too. That's what they called it.

"And how is the football?" he asked, unaware of Rocky's internal monologue. "Nearly time for the quarter-final."

"The football? It's okay," Rocky said, deciding to be open. "But not perfect. There's a funny vibe. Even though we're winning, something is a bit off. I think it's me being captain. But maybe it was a bit like that before. I don't really know. Or get it."

"Are you sure?" Jesse asked.

Rocky didn't get what Jesse was saying. "How do you mean?"

"I mean… is that the case or is it just in your imagination? Do you have proof something is off?"

Rocky shook her head. "It's a vibe. I can feel it. I mean… it might just be in my own mind, but… I don't think so."

There was something in the back of Rocky's mind again. That, since she was made captain, she did tell the other players what to do in training. That she was demanding. But that was right, wasn't it? She was the captain. Weren't captains supposed to lead?

"They don't like being told what to do," Rocky said. "I was made captain and I have to do that. I have to act around other people in ways that I don't like to have done to me. Does that make sense? I am not being very articulate."

Jesse put his hands together, then looked at Rocky.

"You don't like being told what to do? By another player, I mean?"

Rocky remembered Ffion, her captain at Melchester Rovers. Her brother Roy's fiancée now.

Rocky would have done anything for Ffion.

On the pitch. And off it.

She still would.

"I loved it," Rocky said. "I like nothing more than having someone to lead me and to look up to. I mean, it makes life easier, doesn't it? Sometimes…" Rocky paused. There was a funny thought in her head. One of those that kept coming to her recently. "Sometimes," she carried on, "when I have felt really bad—you know, with stuff—I have wished there was a god. Like the kind of god that could tell you this was right and this was wrong and if you did this and didn't do the other then you were okay. And that it was final. There was no debate about it either way."

Rocky stopped. What was she talking about?

Jesse looked straight into her eyes. "I am not going to tell you what to do or what not to do," he said. "I can't. I'm not god either. If there is a god. But I am going to say that you are fifteen and you're at an age where everything changes. Especially with your dad dying and you being away from home. You are changing, excelling even. Your world is changing. And these are good things, necessary things. Try to do what you think is right, but most of all be kind to yourself whether it goes right or wrong."

Rocky closed her eyes. She'd had enough. Her brain was fried. Suddenly Jesse sounded like a priest and she didn't want all that either. But there was something in what he was saying. You could never get everything right, could you? You just had to learn each time you made a mistake, so you made fewer mistakes. Or just didn't make the same ones again.

Too much thinking. Urghhh. Rocky looked at her watch. "I'm off," she said. "Big game tomorrow. Thanks, Jesse."

"Any time, Rocky," Jesse smiled. "Just come to me any time you need to chat. If it helps?"

"It helps," Rocky said, standing. "Thanks again, Jesse."

Then Rocky walked to her apartment.

Tomorrow, she thought. Tomorrow was the quarter-final.

4

GAME DAY.

Rocky took a long slow breath in through her nose, then exhaled through her mouth. She fixed her eyes on the lush green grass at her feet, then on the referee.

This was it, then.

They had had the team talk from Coach Abby. The team was ready. Ready for the game of their lives.

Rocky breathed in again, then out again—slowly, calmly—as the national anthem of the United States of America played over the speakers, listened to by a couple of hundred people there in the small soccer stadium to support the teams.

This was it, then. The game of her life. So far. Was she ready? The question echoed in her head like a mantra to keep her in the place she wanted to be in. As did the answer. Yes, she was ready.

Now Rocky looked around herself, doing a full 360-degree turn. She was with nine other girls wearing white tops and white shorts with a blue and yellow trim. Her keeper—Ella—in green. All wearing the official badge and strip of Mountain Heights School, LA.

Rocky loved their team kit. It reminded her of the new Melchester Rovers away kit, the team she had supported all her life with her mum and dad and brother. The team that her brother played for now in the English top flight for men.

Mountain Heights: her school.

These players: her teammates.

And she was captain.

Another deep breath in, then out.

Captain?

For a half second, as the national anthem continued to play, Rocky's calm thoughts faltered. Did she like being captain? That question in her head again.

Sometimes she felt like it was too much having to be a leader as well as a footballer. Being a leader was weird to Rocky. She had always been a loner. A maverick. Why should ten other girls listen to her? Why couldn't one of the others do that? Let her focus on her game, her private battles on the pitch? And she had a strong feeling that Naomi and Mahsa did not want her to be captain. It was in their body language and glances. But also in what they didn't say or do. No proof of it, like Jesse had asked.

The national anthem went on. As did Rocky's thoughts.

Why am I doing this? Being captain?

The answer was that Abby—their coach— had asked her to do it. Rocky looked up to Abby so much that she would do anything for her. So, Rocky had said yes, she would be captain for her. Just as she would have run through a brick wall for her, crawled the width of America for her.

And here she was.

The match that was about to kick off was the quarter-final of the California State Championship against the Oakland Originals from San Francisco. And it was a big deal. A huge deal.

The most important game Rocky had ever played in.

The furthest any team—girls or boys—had made it in the history of Mountain Heights

School. Ever. In any sport.

Rocky breathed in and out again. Three games from glory. The quarter-final. The semi-final. Then the final. What were the odds? Eight teams. One trophy. That was eight-to-one. A 0.125 chance of winning. Rocky had never been good at maths. But now she was getting better at it.

It was funny how things could change, she thought. Then she tried to get a grip of herself. Her mind was all over the place. And now the national anthem was finished, she needed to get out of her mind and into her body. 'The Star-Spangled Banner'. A decent tune, Rocky thought. A bit more uplifting than 'God Save the King'.

A moment of silence out of respect for the anthem, then shouting and cheers from the small crowd.

"Come on, Mountain Heights!" Rocky

shouted, joining in. "This is it!"

Rocky heard her words echo loudest across the pitch. First hers. Loudest. And that was good, wasn't it? Captains' voices should be loudest, shouldn't they? Then shouts echoing from the mouths of her teammates. Kim, Naomi, Mahsa, Kenzie and the others.

And with every shout—every shout she recognised—Rocky felt more and more like she was in a team. As if in calling out to each other she and her teammates were connecting to each other on invisible threads.

Rocky loved being in a team. Being in this team in particular. Now Rocky, jogging vigorously on the spot, glanced at the referee and saw her lift her whistle to her lips, take a deep breath. Then blow.

Rocky could stop thinking. And start playing.

Kick off!

For the first couple of minutes the quarter-final between Mountain Heights and Oakland Originals was untidy, the ball switching from one team to the other. It was almost as if none of the players—neither team—had the confidence to put their foot on the ball and take control.

Then Rocky saw Naomi lose the ball, having only just won it.

Naomi was normally so solid. But her mind seemed off the game today. Almost as if the importance of the game was so high that she was thinking too much, not playing her natural game.

Rocky decided Naomi needed a kick up the backside. Isn't that what captains did to players under them? It didn't feel right, but Rocky thought it was what she should do.

"Keep to your position, Naomi," Rocky shouted. "Wait for the ball to come to you. You were ball-watching!"

Rocky noticed Naomi glare at her angrily.

Was she angry at Rocky or was she angry at herself? Rocky didn't know for sure. But she knew that she was captain and that part of her job was to call people out. Right?

The game moved on.

Up ahead on the pitch, in the Oakland penalty area, Kim won the ball, her back to goal, and played it back to Rocky in the centre circle. Kim always did this so well. Her back to goal, taking control, keeping possession was one of the most important parts of the shape Mountain Heights took. Everyone knew she might do it and made their runs and took the shape of a team that would play off such a move.

Seamlessly, Rocky ran onto the ball from Kim, controlled it, then moved forward, seeing her wingers run wide, her forwards push on, all onside.

Rocky took in a deep gasp of air.

This was more like it! Mountain Heights were a machine. They knew where they all went and what they would all do. She needed her teammates to play like this every time.

Now she had options. Play it left? Play it right? Run with it?

Rocky chose to play a ball wide to Rachel on the left, then rushed forward with Kenzie and Lexi from her midfield. This was one of their signature moves from deep.

Push on. Fast. Through the heart of the opposition.

Then play it wide and move forward as a unit. A fast attack, the midfielders loading the penalty area along with the forwards. Blitz attack. That's what Abby had called it.

Now a cross from Lexi. She'd taken the ball wide. Maybe too wide, Rocky thought. The best they'd get from this was a corner kick.

The cross ricocheted off an Oakland player behind the goal.

Corner ball.

Rocky had read it right.

"Three and three and three," Rocky shouted, telling her teammates what shape to form.

Three in the box.

Three on the edge of the box.

Three deeper ready to attack if Mountain Heights got the ball, ready to defend if not.

She saw her other winger, Rachel, gather the ball and put it next to the corner flag, then raise one hand, five fingers splayed. This was the secret signal Rocky had devised as captain for a deep corner.

Rocky backed off, found some space. There was a one-in-three chance the ball would break to her, she figured.

A thirty-three per cent chance.

Maths. Or math as they called it here in the US. What was the matter with her? Thinking about the classroom when she was on the pitch playing football? She had spent her life in the classroom thinking about football.

The corner came across, just skimming off Kim and then Beth's head before being hoofed away hard by a defender. The ball bounced, spinning into the space in front of Rocky. And Rocky ran at it.

She had this.

Rocky took the ball the first time, controlling it with her left knee, then her right boot, and attacking.

The Oakland players were backing off. She could tell they feared her. And knew that was half her job. Make the opposition wary of you. They might have seen footage of how Mountain Heights played. They might even have watched her doing this. That direct thrust at a defence. Causing chaos. So hard to defend against. The fear you might give away a free kick—or, worse, a penalty—if the player made it into the box.

Running hard and fast at the left-hand side of the Oakland defence, Rocky knew that Rebecca would be filling the gap she was creating to the right and her two forwards would be making angled runs into the penalty area, making sure they were not offside.

She looked up. Yes. They were all there. The machine was in working order.

Perfect.

And Oakland were still backing off.

Even better.

Yes, nobody liked a midfielder willing to run hard at a defence with power. And Rocky was that midfielder. Ripping at the opposition. Testing them out.

No tackle came in. Rocky found herself

inside the D, hyperaware that Mahsa was running in an arc into space just behind her.

Rocky feinted to shoot, saw the keeper and defenders shape for her shot, ready to leap to save it or throw a leg out to block it, just get something on the ball. But Rocky didn't blast the ball as the opposition players around her had anticipated. Instead, she side-footed the ball with a delicate flick between two cautious Oakland defenders to Mahsa.

Mahsa's first touch took her deep into the penalty area, wide right, and her second touch left her wheeling away, arms raised as the ball angled into the net.

Goal. Six minutes in. Mountain Heights 1, Oakland Originals nil.

The perfect start to the quarter-final of the California State Championship.

Now Rocky heard herself shouting.

"Get back. Back into our half. Get that

shape back. Come on. There are eighty-plus minutes of soccer to go. Come on!"

5

ROCKY FELT AN arm around her shoulder as she jogged back to the penalty spot for the restart of the quarter-final.

Normally she hated anyone hugging her, putting an arm around her, even touching her. But this arm was okay.

"Did you just hear yourself?" Kim was laughing. As were Beth and Kenzie.

Rocky frowned. "Hear what?" What was going on? Why was her team laughing? She almost felt like calling them out, telling them to focus and stop being silly. She was glad she had not. She didn't want to sound like a teacher.

"What you just said?" Kim carried on, still grinning.

"What?" Rocky said again, rewinding to her last words, trying to work it out.

There are eighty-plus minutes of soccer to go.

Soccer...

Had she really said that?

No. No, she couldn't have. And now Rocky was laughing, too.

She'd said it at last.

Soccer!

There was this joke among her Mountain Heights teammates. How Rocky always called soccer football. How she was English and she used the English word for the game. Like 'pitch' instead of 'field', 'boots' instead of 'cleats', 'draw' instead of 'tie'.

Her teammates had been waiting months for this. The day that Rocky Race said 'soccer' would be a day for celebration. And lots of laughter.

Today was the day.

Rocky laughed along. She knew that this was good for her team. Because it was good for the opposition to see you laughing as a team, wasn't it?

It showed team spirit.

It showed confidence.

It was hard to face a team with confidence and team spirit.

But Rocky—deep down in the core of her being—was cross with herself. She had wanted never to say soccer, always to say football. To prove that the English way—her way—was the right way.

But now?

Now she had as good as accepted the game she loved was called soccer. The American word for it.

Most of the Mountain Heights team were American and, to them, it had always been soccer. All American, except Mahsa who was from Iran and Naomi who was from Ghana. And Rocky. And football in the States was American football. All padding and helmets to Rocky. She didn't understand it. In fact, she went out of her way to appear confused about it. Even though one of her and Kim's best friends was Cody, star player of the Mountain Heights American football team. Especially because of that. To wind him up.

Despite living in the US for nine months, Rocky had never said soccer. Until now. Win or lose this game, Rocky knew she was going to get teased for that slip.

We'd better win then, she said to herself, as Oakland restarted the match. *We need to win. If I'm captain. It's on me, isn't it?*

And there it was again. That pressure. One-nil up and she was still tense. Really tense. When did you stop being anxious about a football match when you were captain? Did you have to be four-nil ahead with ten minutes to go before you could enjoy it? She remembered worrying about Kim leaving to take a pro contract. And how the more she enjoyed being best friends with Kim, the more she felt anxious about when it would end. Just like this game.

Stop thinking ahead, Rocky said to herself. *Focus*.

"Come on," she shouted. "Focus!" As much to herself as her teammates.

Rocky rolled her eyes at herself and sighed. Her team had scored a goal and her first thought was What if we concede? What if our lead doesn't last five minutes? We need another. Then another.

For the next half an hour the football was what Rocky called safe football. Both teams getting the measure of the other after the shock of the opening goal.

Safe.

Mountain Heights not needing to take risks with a one-goal lead.

Safe.

Oakland not wanting to concede a second and be too far behind to mount a comeback.

It would be better to call it tense football.

But, as the game went on and the adrenaline of the opening goal faded, Rocky realised that 'safe' could mean calm, 'safe' could mean control, that she and her teammates could afford to play the game in a lower gear. Conserve their energy. So many teams lost the game in the last quarter because they had worn themselves out in the first half. Rocky knew that her Mountain Heights team were fit, but there was always the fear that the opposition were fitter.

One day a team would be fitter than them. By the law of averages it had to happen.

Maths again. Math. Why was she always thinking in terms of what was once her least favourite subject?

Law of averages.

Quarters.

Halves.

Percentages.

One goal.

Two goals. What was happening to her? It was almost as if she liked that sort of thing. Or that it actually meant something now.

But a two-goal lead would be nice, she thought to herself.

And the chance for that came. Just before half time.

Mountain Heights won a free kick on the

edge of the penalty area. A result of Kim having her shirt pulled as she tried to get on the end of a Rocky through ball.

Rocky knew this was a key moment. Score now and Oakland would be broken. Two–nil at half time meant you had to score three in the second half. More maths!

Rocky grabbed the ball. Even if the Oakland team were fitter than Mountain Heights, they'd have to be very fit to do that. Rocky took control. She felt like being firm. Like being bossy. She had this. They had this. She barked out instructions. They were here to win, weren't they? And she knew how.

"Kim. Beth. Rebecca. One of you is taking it. Lexi, Kenzie and Rachel, on the edge of the area for the rebound. The rest of us, behind the ball."

Rocky stepped back, glad to have a chance to stand for a moment as the Oakland players formed a defensive wall. She watched her players do what she'd asked and smiled. They were such a great team. Some of them had their weaknesses, but, as a team, they were great.

The machine. Her machine.

And they listened to Rocky. At least she thought they did. It felt like they did. And they didn't resent her being so bossy, did they? Was it even bossy? It was captainy, wasn't it? Was captainy even a word?

It was weird that they listened to her. At the beginning of being captain, Rocky was unsure even about asking players to do something on the pitch.

How did you do it right?

Would you mind dropping back to defend when we've lost the ball, thank you?

Please can you take throw ins and not leave it to Kenzie?

Things like that. She'd be too polite and it didn't sound right. She tried to listen to Abby coaching them and be more Abby. Abby demanded things of players. If she said jump, they would jump. Rocky would jump.

I need you back in defence now.

Take the throw in. Don't leave it.

That was more like it.

But when it came to free kicks, Rocky knew to leave that to her strike partnership, Kim and Beth. Kim being the other best player. And scoring goals was not Rocky's strong point.

Rocky stepped back and watched Kim and Beth talk, hands covering their mouths. Then she saw Kim back up in preparation to take a run at the ball, Beth standing slightly aside. And Rocky wondered if Kim was going to hit it to the right of the wall or was she trying to fool the keeper and Beth was going to put it round the left of the wall?

The ref blew her whistle.

Beth seemed to move, maybe ready to shoot.

Then Kim was on it, blasting the ball round the wall, a curve in the shot, sudden and shocking, the net billowing.

A huge cheer.

Kim and Beth hugging. Players mobbing them. 2-0 up in the quarterfinal of the California State Championship! This was unbelievable!

Rocky went over to Beth, then Kim, feeling a strange twinge of discomfort that Kim's arm was round Beth and not her. What was that about? Then shaking the stupid feeling away, focusing on the team. The game. The championship.

"Come on!" Rocky called out to the rest of the Mountain Heights team. "We need to focus. Keep it at nil until half time. We're never more vulnerable to concede than after we score. I need focus. Come on!"

6

WHEN THE FINAL whistle went in the quarter-final of the California State Championship, Rocky and her teammates gathered at the side of the pitch with their coaches, Abby and Jesse. After shaking hands with the Oakland Originals players, of course.

A 2–1 win.

Tight at the end after Oakland had got a goal back in the seventy-first minute. It had been close to going into extra time, but Mountain Heights had held on for the win. Just.

The atmosphere among Rocky and her

teammates was amazing. One of excitement. But also one of relief.

Kim was beaming. Rocky hadn't seen her this happy for months. She seemed so carefree when she was involved in football. It was her escape.

But Rocky knew Kim wasn't carefree. How could she be?

This was her first thought after she had gone and congratulated all her teammates and commiserated with the players from the team they had just beaten.

Should it be? she wondered. Was that the right thing?

As her teammates chatted, Rocky's thoughts were on Kim. Not the victory. She knew she should be enjoying this, but no... as usual... her mind had taken her in a different direction.

Then she had an idea. Rocky wondered if she could get the team to do a cool-down run for ten, even fifteen minutes, just to keep Kim on the pitch and engaged in football. Rocky wondered if her best friend's mind wandered like hers did during and after a match. All those thoughts that had been in Rocky's head during the match! The stuff to do with maths and with being a captain: did that happen to other people? Was Kim thinking about her mum being ill like Rocky constantly thought about her dad being ill before? Or was it just Rocky?

Abby led a short team talk, a huddle at the side of the pitch. Rocky listened carefully. They'd done well, Abby said. But nearly let it slip with that late goal in the seventy-first minute. In the future they really had to take their chances and put a team to the sword, Abby said, and make sure that conceding a random late goal against the run of play wasn't so significant.

Then Abby mentioned that there had been scouts watching. From professional clubs in the US. There to look for young players to take on as future professionals.

There were gasps and eyes flashing with excitement.

"I instructed them not to speak to any of you, nor to me," Abby explained. "But they were watching some of you, I know. I think it is only fair to let you know that."

"Watching Kim and Rocky," Naomi said.

There was a laugh. Everyone knew that Kim and Rocky were the two players scouts would most likely come to watch.

"And you," Rocky said to Naomi.

"Yeah, sure," Naomi said sarcastically.

"You must be so excited," Ella, the keeper, interrupted what could have become a tricky conversation. "Do you think you'll go pro, Kim? Give up college?"

Aware that Abby was watching them talk about the scouts, Rocky saw Kim grin with excitement. Well, that was her dream, wasn't it?

Now Rocky began to worry about her friend again.

Because Kim looked confused about what she should say, maybe even think.

"Let's not focus on scouts," Rocky interjected. "All we should be thinking about is the semi-final next Saturday. There's so much going on in the world that the last thing we should be worrying about is scouts."

Ella looked chastened. "Yeah. God. Sorry."

Rocky felt her eyes well up. This was crazy. Then she noticed Abby was watching her. Could Abby see inside Rocky's mind? Did she know everything? Sometimes Rocky looked up to Abby so much she wouldn't be surprised. What was the word their English

Literature teacher had used? Omniscience? That was it. Some people thought God had omniscience. That he—if he was a he—was all-seeing.

Rocky shook her head. She was thinking about her studies again. What was happening to her?

"All I can say is that the scouts can watch, but not approach any of you," Abby said. "Not until we are out of the state championship."

Abby had changed the course of the conversation as if she really was reading Rocky's mind. Whether she was omniscient or not, Rocky was grateful.

Rocky tried to help her move the conversation on.

"Out?" Rocky asked, half joking. "We're not going out! We're going to win it! Kim's gonna score a hat-trick in the final."

Abby smiled. "I was hoping you'd say that."

Then another silence. A handful of the girls glancing from Abby to Rocky to Kim, then each other. Naomi staring quite obviously. A weird silence. Rocky could sense something. That the vibe was off, like she'd said to Jesse. There was something. But what was it?

Was it something she had said? Was she being bossy? Was she sucking up to Abby? Or was it because she was favouring Kim? Bigging her up? Everyone knew Kim and Rocky were tight.

Rocky decided not to suggest the cool-down run. They'd only think she was sucking up to Abby again.

Rocky looked at Kim once more. That bewildered look was still there. What was she thinking? About the game? Or about her whole football career, the scouts and all that? To move towards being a pro footballer or to stay at school? Was that what was in her mind?

Instantly Rocky changed her mind and turned to Abby. "I think we should do a cool-down run, Abby. Just a few laps of the pitch. Start the recovery now for the semi next week."

Rocky heard a few mumbles of disagreement. Her team wanted to hit the showers, then see their family who'd been watching on the bleachers. Rocky knew that. But she had also seen Kim nod and start stretching in preparation. So, she decided to press for it.

"Two laps," Rocky said. "Come on. This will give us that extra one per cent next week. It might make the difference."

"Go on," Abby agreed. "Two laps. Listen to your captain. Nice and steady. Half pace at most. It's not a race to get to the dressing room any sooner."

"I'm not sure—" Naomi started to say.

But Kim stepped forward. "Come on. Two laps, Naomi."

And Naomi gave way. To Kim. Everyone gave way to Kim. She was the golden girl. Rocky knew that. Liked that. Maybe, Rocky thought, Kim should be captain?

After some glances and grumbles, the Mountain Heights team set off slowly on two laps of the pitch. Some more reluctantly than others.

Rocky joined Kim at the back.

They didn't talk, and Rocky was unable to stop her mind going round and round with thoughts about whether she really wanted to be a captain to this team at all.

Part Two:
Semi-Final

7

THE FIRST TRAINING session after the quarter-final win was not on the football field, nor in the gym. It was in a classroom!

It felt different. And it was different. There was a semi-final to be played. One that, if they won it, meant they would be in the California State Championship final.

Abby stood at the front of the room in front of a big screen. Jesse waited at the side of the room, closing the blinds, so that the evening sun, coming in at an angle from the west over the Pacific, didn't shine on the screen and obscure their viewing.

"When I was with Team USA," Abby began, "we would watch videos of all the teams we played. Why do you think that was, girls?"

Rocky's hand shot up. She was bursting with energy and excitement about being in the semi-finals. She answered without being asked to speak. "To know how they played," she said. "To work out each player's strengths and weaknesses. All that."

"That's it," Abby nodded. "What else?"

Rocky shot her hand up again. And again didn't wait for the nod from their coach. "To see what their set pieces were like. Corners. Free kicks. Even throw ins."

Abby looked around the room. No other hands had gone up. She narrowed her eyes.

"Naomi?" Abby said. "What do you think?"

"What Rocky said," Naomi replied.

Rocky glanced at her roommate. She was changing. Definitely. More confident. But then Kim had said the same of Rocky. They were all changing. People did.

"And," Rocky added, "so we can think about our weaknesses. Identify them. Own them. So that we can see where they can hurt us. And…"

Rocky heard her voice trail off. She sounded just like one of those clever kids in class who liked the sound of their own voice. *Miss! Miss! I know. Ask me.*

What was happening to her? Was she changing too much? Was she annoying? Should she keep her mouth shut? She had always hated clever talkative people in class. But it was different in football.

Wasn't it?

Maybe it wasn't.

Now Rocky got why she was so troubled by this. This was football, yes. But they were in a classroom. And so she was coming across as a classroom clever clogs, or whatever her gran used to say.

"Anyone else?" Abby asked.

No replies. Rocky had been too eager, talking too much again. But it was only because she was so excited. Wasn't it? She had more to say, but managed to keep her mouth shut. Or should she say more? She was captain. Didn't captains lead? Didn't they fill in the silences?

"Right," Abby smiled. "Fine. There will be more to talk about once we have watched this. Please have your notebooks at the ready."

Their coach turned to look at the screen that was frozen with the heading 'San Diego Sundowns v Salinas Pearls'.

Abby tapped the frame of the screen. "I want you to study the San Diego Sundowns. Make some notes. Particularly the players you'll come up against in your positions. Mahsa and Naomi, study their centre forwards. Kim and Beth, look at how their defence plays offside. Okay?"

Rocky said nothing. She knew she was the only one talking and she still felt there was a weird vibe with the other girls in the team.

When had that started? In training? During the quarter-final? And was it about Rocky? Or was it about something else and she was being paranoid? Or had she done something off the pitch? Something the whole of the school knew or thought about her? Was it Kim? Was it her and Kim staying together all Easter?

Rocky stared at her notebook and pen. So many questions. What were the answers? Were there any?

Rocky's mind was searching for answers. And, instead of saying anything more, she chose to stare at the screen, to wait for Abby to press play.

"Be sure to make a note of the time on screen if there's something you want us to come back to," Abby added.

Silence.

"Hello?" Abby said. "Anyone there?"

"Yes, Coach," Rocky said reluctantly.

Abby had wanted a response. She had got one.

Now Abby pressed play. And they watched.

San Diego were good. Their offside trap was slick. Four defenders working like they were on the highest difficulty setting on a video game. They played a high line. And they pressed, meaning the opposition never got much time on the ball. A second and they'd close you down. To play against them you had to be quick thinking and accurate. Or you'd lose the ball. Lose a goal. Even lose the game.

San Diego were also very physical. They'd

push, nudge, even tug at hair. Rocky watched, her face forming a sneer of dislike for the team that was between Mountain Heights and the final of the California State Championship.

"Okay," Abby said, when she switched off the video. "What thoughts do you have?"

Rocky felt eyes on her. Like everyone was assuming she would speak. She had lots to say. One thing in particular. But, having felt that funny vibe, she decided to wait.

Now Kim put her hand up.

"Kim?" Abby said.

"They play a high line. When Lexi or Rebecca are working the ball through from the wings or when Rock passes from deep, we need to synchronise perfectly. That team they were playing were offside," Kim checked her notebook, "eighteen times."

"Good," Abby said. "And we can work on that in training. What else?"

Rachel's arm went up after another silence. "They crowd the penalty area. Block the keeper. They push defenders into the keeper. So they foul, but it's indirect. Hard for the ref."

"Excellent," Abby said. "Yes. We need to protect Ella. She will be a target, especially at set pieces. They'll be up to all sorts of tricks. You see they won the penalty that led to their winning goal by causing the defending team to be frustrated and angry in the penalty area."

Silence.

"We need to be so careful in the box," Jesse added after a few moments.

More silence.

Rocky was becoming increasingly frustrated. Her teammates were not engaging with this. It reminded her of how she used to be in class. Head down. No answers. Because her mind was on something else. Or because she was scared of saying something stupid or being called a teacher's pet for answering anything at all.

But she was the talker now. Mostly.

She felt Abby's eyes on her. Like Abby needed help from her. And something snapped in Rocky's head. Why should she be quiet? When Rachel had said she dominated she had understood it as a criticism. Now she was happy to take it as a compliment. She'd be the teacher's pet. Fine.

"Everything we are talking about," Rocky said. "Well, most of it. It's about what San Diego do without the ball. Everything is about catching us offside, forcing us to lose the ball. It's all negative."

"Good," Abby said. "What else?"

"They're dirty," Rocky went on. "They foul. Cynical nudges. Pushing. Nothing big, but enough to unbalance the opposition. And to get inside our heads. Come on." Rocky turned round and made her chair scrape the floor. "Didn't you see it?"

No reply.

Rocky went on. "They press. They don't give you a minute on the ball. You don't have time to think. They want to be in your head. One on one they badger you all game, get in your way. Trash talk you. It's ugly. They rely on free kicks, deep throw ins, corners. That penalty. That's why they scored. And they thrive on breaking down passing moves. They can't play with the ball, so they stop their opposition playing with the ball instead."

Rocky looked at Abby.

"Exactly. That's it. Anyone else?"

No one spoke. Not even Kim. Rocky felt like pulling at her own hair in frustration.

"How much possession do you think they

had?" Rocky stood up and faced the class. "How much of the ball?"

Kim suggested forty percent.

No one else spoke.

Should I even be captain? Rocky asked herself. *They clearly have no respect for me.*

She hated this. Suddenly she preferred being the Rocky who sat at the back of the class and said nothing. And did nothing. And now she was going on and on, analysing the other team. Even analysing poetry. What had happened to her?

"Mahsa? Naomi?" Rocky put her two housemates on the spot. "How much do you think?"

Mahsa looked at the floor. She was never one for putting her hand up. Naomi looked fiercely at Rocky.

"You tell us," Naomi said.

Rocky was shocked to see both her

housemates were looking back at her like they were cross. And she had no idea why. Not really.

"I had it down as less than twenty-five percent," Rocky said, hearing herself going on and on because she had to, because she was captain. "San Diego don't play football. They play anti-football. And we need to be a tight team together or we have no chance against them."

Rocky looked at all her teammates.

"A team," she said more quietly.

8

KIM AND ROCKY were sitting in the communal room of their dorm. Both were on their mobiles. Or cell phones. Depending on who you asked.

While reflecting on the weirdness in her friendship group and team, Rocky remembered the week the four girls—Rocky, Kim, Mahsa and Naomi—had first met.

The four had got along so well they all opted to share a flat.

They were known by some as the fab four.

But maybe not any more.

How did that happen? A subtle change

somewhere among a group of friends and the whole thing doesn't feel right. And, in addition, you are too scared to talk to one of the group about it because it might make things worse.

But why? Why had it changed?

She went back to the beginning. How they had been. What they were like. If they were different now.

The girls were definitely all different from the start, Rocky remembered. Well, she and Kim were a bit alike. Both obsessed with football. Both with dreams of being a professional player, of playing in the World Cup for their country. Kim for the USA. Rocky for England.

Mahsa and Naomi were at Mountain Heights for the football. Yes. They were good at it. They worked hard at it. They had been quite similar to each other too, in some ways.

Their priority was education.

Not something Rocky had bothered about. Until recently.

And both were quiet early in the school year, though Naomi was becoming more strident now. But that was normal. At the beginning of anything people are shy. They might not be completely themselves, not wanting to give too much away, not wanting to annoy other people, so they try to be normal. Whatever that meant. Rocky wondered if she should have been more like that. But she was never good at pretending. She hated pretence. Unless someone had a good reason for it.

Rocky remembered that—at first—she could not work out why Mahsa and Naomi bothered with school work. Why they lived in the library, surrounded by books.

And then—last term—Rocky had nearly left school because she couldn't cope with studying. It was Mahsa and Naomi who had helped her. Along with Jesse. And they said to her they couldn't understand how she didn't want to be educated.

But, even with such differences, the four girls had become close. Really close. They had each other's back.

Until now.

Now it was weird. Since Easter, it had been weird.

Why?

Rocky lay on her bed and tried to think what had changed.

She had been made captain.

That was one thing.

She had stayed in the US over Easter—at Kim's house.

That was another.

And she and Kim were closer now. So, it wasn't four equals in a group like it had been at the beginning. But Naomi and Mahsa had always been even closer, hadn't they?

And so what? Rocky thought.

What was she supposed to do?

Aaaarghh, what was the answer?

Was she meant to analyse her friendships, work out the problems and solve them? How did you do that? And anyway, Rocky had never had that many friends. This was unusual for her. To have a best friend. To have two other close friends. To be in a team—a squad—of twenty girls, all reliant on each other.

Rocky was out of her depth.

And out of her depth most of all because she had been made captain.

Maybe that was it. Did everyone behave differently towards you as soon as you were a leader?

Maybe.

Or was it the Kim thing?

Why would Naomi and Mahsa—and the others in the team—be so weird about her and Kim being close? They were close, too. Mahsa and Naomi were always in the library, studying together.

Rocky felt a rush of anger now.

So that was fine? Yeah! What about that? Two girls being close because they shared a love of studying? Why was it not okay for Kim and Rocky to be close? They had something in common. Something bigger than their friendship. Or studying. Even bigger than football.

Cancer.

How about that?

Rocky rolled her eyes. She knew she was overthinking it now. But it felt good. She felt better to have found a reason to be angry. How dare anyone be cross with them for having a dad who had died of cancer and a mum who still had cancer?

Enough of that!

Snapping out of her thoughts, Rocky almost got up to go and confront Mahsa and Naomi. Storm over to their room. Bang on the door. Stride in. They could have it out. Right there.

"I want to have it out with Mahsa and Naomi," Rocky said across the sitting room.

"You sure?" Kim asked. "I mean, it might be good to leave it alone. I'll back you all the way, but isn't it good for everyone just to sleep on it?"

"My mum says you should never go to bed with an unfinished argument."

"But you haven't had an argument," Kim said. "Yet."

The two friends laughed. Loudly. Because they were nervous. Just as Naomi and Mahsa appeared through the door.

Mahsa smiled and said good night in a soft voice. But Naomi didn't smile. She had her hands on her hips.

Rocky had no idea what was going on. So, she went for it. Anything would be better than not knowing. Not doing anything.

It was time.

"What's going on, Naomi?" she asked.

Mahsa made to return to her room. But Rocky wanted her there. It was really Naomi she wanted to have it out with, but still.

"Mahsa?" Rocky asked. "Please can you stay?"

Rocky held Naomi's stare. Five seconds. Ten seconds. The room felt like it was going to explode, and she looked away first. She felt panic rising. She felt sick. She felt a huge urge to be in her bedroom at home in Melchester.

"Is there any point?" Naomi said in a low voice.

"In what?" Kim persisted.

"In talking with Rocky. Shouldn't we just listen to her?"

Rocky felt a surge of anger now. But she put her hands up. In surrender.

"Whatever I've done, I'm sorry," she said.

"That's the thing, Rocky," Mahsa said now. "You don't know what you've done. You might as well say I'm sorry you feel that way about what I've done."

Rocky felt her stomach cramp. What was going on? These were two of her best friends. Nice people. Calm people. Good people. But they were cross with her.

Rocky could see lights around her peripheral vision. She wondered if she was having a stroke. *No, don't be ridiculous,* she said to herself. *This is panic. This is anxiety. You need to get out of here.*

Rocky lifted herself out of the chair. "I

don't understand this. I can't handle this," she said. "Good night. Nobody follow me. Please. I'll see you all tomorrow."

Then she turned, opened her door, didn't switch the light on, closed the door again, careful not to slam it because that was aggressive, went over to her bin and threw up her dinner.

Rocky lay on her bed as the light outside faded and night fell. Her mind was on fire. Her room smelled of bile. She had gone through so many feelings and plans and ideas in one night. From wanting to attack, wanting to give up, feeling energised and feeling defeated. All in no time at all. How did you process that? All while wondering what the hell people thought of you, even more than caring what you thought of them.

And she listened to the other girls.

There was an argument going on. Naomi

attacking Rocky. Kim defending her. Mahsa silent. Sometimes the argument was in quiet voices, occasionally voices were raised.

But Rocky could only hear phrases. Fragments. Not whole arguments. Still, she tried to make sense of them.

"Who does she think she is, bossing us around?" Naomi.

"She's a leader on the pitch, but not off it." Naomi again.

Then Kim fighting back. "She's grown more confident, so what? Isn't that what happens when you practise?" And, "Isn't she a good leader? Aren't we winning because of her?"

Naomi retaliated. "But that is all she is interested in. Winning. It's not fun any more. She bosses us about."

Now Mahsa's voice. Rocky heard it clear and calm and it chilled her. "And she only wants to win for herself, so she can get a pro contract. Then she'll go. Leave us. Leave you, Kim. How would you like that?"

"I'd be happy for her," Kim said.

"Kim's going to get a pro contract," Naomi said to Mahsa. "She's the one who's leaving."

A silence. A long one. Rocky could only hear herself breathing and a plane going overhead. She imagined it was going to England and she wished she was on it, looking down on California and knowing she was not coming back. That would be nice. Forget the dilemma of staying at Mountain Heights versus joining a pro team if they came to scout you. Forget her growing fear that her best friend would have the best news—a pro contract—and would leave her alone at Mountain Heights.

"And there's school work," Mahsa was complaining. "I am spending too much time on football. This used to be fun."

"And then there was Easter," Naomi said aggressively. Or so loudly that she hoped Rocky might hear.

"What about Easter?" Kim shot back. "Oh that... So she stayed with me? You went home. Both of you. Rocky didn't. She was supporting me. Remember?"

Then it went quiet again.

Rocky had never heard Kim use her mum's illness in an argument or to get sympathy. She had kept it really low key. She was adamant she would not do that. Until now. And—hearing it—Rocky couldn't help but smile. That her friend would go against what she wanted to do to defend her.

Rocky stood up and moved to the door. She was ready to get stuck in now. Two-footed. She felt like she was on the pitch and about to take someone out and be given a red card and for it to be worth it.

Red mist.

She loved the red mist. You left all your doubts and troubles behind when the red mist came down. Even though you knew that—after you did whatever you did—things would be worse. At the time red mist was a joy.

Because she had been moving across the room and because she knocked her bin over, and stumbled to see her sick from earlier on the carpet now, she missed part of the conversation. On her knees, in pain, she heard the end of it.

"That's not kind." Kim was speaking. "Why would you think that? Look. My mom's sick. Sick is bad, but she will live. Rocky's dad died. She is still grieving. Can't you tell?"

Something else from Naomi.

Then Kim again. "Yes, I know it was over a year ago that he died. But is your dad dead?

Do you know how long it takes to get over it? I don't. My parents are both still alive. And yours are too. Lucky me. Lucky you. Unlucky Rocky. What if you never get over it?"

Rocky got up off the floor and turned back to drag herself onto her bed, then buried herself under the cover and sobbed.

Doors slammed. A text arrived. From Kim.

Going to sleep. Text if you need me. Love you. K xxx

Rocky didn't reply.

9

ROCKY COULD NOT sleep. The argument between Kim and Mahsa and Naomi had flooded her with adrenaline and thoughts that she could not process.

And there was the semi-final tomorrow. What sort of preparation was this?

And all the things that had been said were competing in her head as if the argument was still going on.

She bosses us around.

She only wants to win for herself, so she can get a pro contract.

What about Easter?

My mom will live; Rocky's dad died.

Do you know how long it takes to get over it?

What if you never get over it?

It was all there. So many things to worry about.

That the other girls didn't like her. They thought that she was bossing them about. And it was not just Naomi and Mahsa thinking that. Clearly. Were they all talking about her behind her back? She thought they were a unit. But maybe she was bossy. Maybe she was spoiling everything.

And then there was that they all thought she was only there to get a professional contract. Was that even true? What if it was? What if she was utterly selfish and it was all about her? How could you know?

Then Easter. Had Mahsa and Naomi been funny about Rocky spending Easter with Kim? Were they jealous? And what were they jealous of? So what if they were closer than the other girls? They needed each other.

Rocky opened her eyes. Did she? Did she need Kim? And what did that mean?

Then—thinking back to the conversation—the bombshell at the end. Kim saying that even though her mum was ill, the fact that Rocky's dad was dead was worse still.

Was it?

And was she still grieving?

So many questions. Her head felt like it was going to burst and she could see little lights around the edges of her vision again.

And it was not just these questions for Rocky to deal with. But the lack of answers, too.

Rocky picked up her phone and looked at Kim's text again.

Text if you need me.
Love you.

Rocky wanted to reply, but she wanted Kim to sleep more. The match tomorrow. She refused to keep Kim awake. She thrived on a good night's sleep before a match.

Rocky wondered if she should call her mum instead. It was nine in the evening here. It'd be five in the morning in Melchester.

No. She didn't want to wake Mum.

Rocky looked at the other text she'd had from home. Her brother. Sending a picture of an article on the BBC website with a laughing with tears emoji.

TYNECASTER HIT WITH MASSIVE POINTS DEDUCTION

Melchester are back as the city's no. 1 team

She had to smile. Here was Roy Race—

the Premier League footballer, the legend—
sending comedy texts like that.

Suddenly Rocky welled up.

Roy.

The famous footballer.

But he was also her brother.

She picked up her phone again.

Texted.

Rocky: You up?

Roy: Yeah. Off for a walk. With next door's dog, Bamford. His owners are away. It's lovely out.

Rocky: Can we call?

Roy: Sure. Just getting Bamford then will call. xxx

WHEN ROY CALLED, Rocky could hear the

morning noises of where they lived. Next door's gate shutting. The birds in the trees. The sound of the odd car going down the hill into town. She felt a deep stab of homesickness. And the idea of going home appealed. A lot.

"So, what's up?" Roy asked. "Are you okay?"

"Not really. Just a bit… you know."

"Talk to me."

"It's stupid, I don't even want to put it into words. But I wanted to ask you two questions. They've been going round my head all day and I was going to talk to Mum, but I don't want to worry her and I reckon you can give me better answers."

"Hit me," Roy said.

Rocky couldn't not laugh. "If you'd have said that face to face when we were kids…"

"… you would have hit me," Roy laughed, too. "So, what are your questions?"

"You got made captain, right?"

"Yeah. Years ago."

"Did you like it? I mean, at first?"

Roy hesitated. "No. It took some getting used to."

"Yeah?"

"Yeah. Listen, you're captain now, aren't you?"

"I am."

"Struggling?"

"I don't like it. I either don't say anything or I say too much. Or I say stuff off the pitch and they don't like me being bossy. I'm not sure. They don't say."

"Talk to your coach. He can help you— she," Roy spluttered. "Sorry. My bad. Talk to her. Your coach."

"Hmmm."

"And if you don't like it, give it up."

Rocky swallowed. *Give it up? Was it as simple as that?* She nearly laughed. Was Roy

121

saying she didn't have to be captain? It was like… what did you call it?… a lightbulb moment? When there's a choice you can make, an option you can take, that could help you out of a hole.

"Is it affecting how you play?" Roy pressed on.

"I think so," Rocky admitted.

"Then at least tell your coach that."

"Thanks, Roy." Rocky could hear her brother was on the top of the hill now. The wind in his phone sounded like the roar of some wild animal. "How's the view?"

"Good," Roy said. "Bamford! Leave that. Don't eat… oh."

"How's Bamford?" Rocky asked.

"He's good. Apart from his taste in… I'll spare you the detail. So, what was your second question?"

Rocky swallowed. She listened to the wind

at home, buffeting Roy's phone. The wind that used to wuther her window frame at night. Lovely. She'd like to be back in her bedroom at home.

"When does grieving for Dad get easier?" she said, surprising herself.

More wind howling.

Roy laughed. "You know, I was just going to ask you that at Christmas. It seems to be getting harder for me."

And then they were both laughing. Rocky felt better. A bit better.

"Remind me why we're laughing," Rocky asked.

"Beats me," her brother replied.

"I miss home. Mum," Rocky said. "I even miss you."

"You must be struggling," he responded.

More laughing, tears coming down Rocky's face.

This felt good. Really good. Rocky remembered home and Mum and having a big brother who looked out for her and loved her even if she was always trying to annoy him. Swept up in the emotion of that comfort, she half felt like telling her brother that she wanted to give up Mountain Heights and come home... when he interrupted her thoughts.

"I reckon me and Mum should come out and see you," he said.

"I'd love that!" Rocky sat up. What a great idea.

"Let me talk to Mum. The season finishes here soon and we have until July off. Maybe a trip to the States?"

"Please," Rocky said.

A pause. Just the wind and Bamford barking at something.

"I miss him," Roy said, breaking the silence.

"Dad."

"I do too," Rocky said.

"You know, one thing I miss is him saying he is proud of us. Do you remember how that used to feel?"

Rocky nodded. Then tried to say yes, but a sob stopped her.

"You need to know," Roy said slowly, as if it was painful to get the words out, "with him not here to tell you, that I am really proud of you, Rocky. And that he would be too."

10

ROCKY HAD A very fixed pre-match routine—
and it began the moment she woke up on
match day.

Six-fifty a.m. alarm, then into the bathroom.
Which was always free before seven.

This meant she could get to breakfast first
at half-past seven, sit at a table with her
pancakes and with a view over the hills with
her back to the dining area, meaning she
didn't have to talk to anyone or even look at
anyone until at least eight, when she got back
to her dorm.

It worked every match day.

Except today.

Rocky heard the sound of someone in the shared bathroom even before she put her hand on the door handle. One of the others was in the shower.

"No way," she said. What was going on? No one ever used the bathroom this early.

She waited with her towel tucked under her arm, slumped in one of the sofas, her mind going over and over the terrible night she had had after talking to Roy, after all the carry on with the others.

Waking up to check the clock at 00:15, 01:23, 03:11 and more. Had she slept in? Of course not. She never slept in. And suffering half dreams in her head that she wasn't sure were dreams or scenarios she had made up or even memories.

A glass being slammed down on a table, orange juice splashing everywhere. Her standing up and saying I'm leaving. I'm going home.

A sinkhole appearing in the football pitch and Rocky falling into it, then looking back up to see everyone staring down at her.

And Abby had been there for both.

Strange dream, indeed.

Mahsa came out of the bathroom, at last.

Rocky tried to fade her impatient scowl and smile.

"Morning, Mahsa," she said.

"Good morning," Mahsa said with a half smile, but not a full smile, nor a real smile. Rocky looked at her. Was she being unfriendly, guarded?

"You okay?" Rocky asked. She really meant, Are we okay? but it felt too direct to ask that.

Mahsa shrugged and looked at Naomi's door. Half smiled again.

Weirdness. There was definitely weirdness.

"Big game today," Rocky said, squirming.

What was going on? She was making uncomfortable conversation with one of her housemates.

"Yeah," Mahsa said. Then she slipped into her room, the door closing ever so softly behind her.

Rocky hit the bathroom. The smile she had made to Mahsa's remark stuck on her face even when she looked at herself in the mirror and heard a voice. *You don't want to be captain. You wish Naomi was captain. Anyone. Anyone but you. You are dreading today.*

No.

Enough.

Enough of this.

She should crack on with the day as she had wanted to. It was so early in the morning any conversation was going to be stilted. They were teenage girls. She knew that teenage girls could be funny in the morning. Just like teenage boys and middle-aged men and women could be. Everyone could be funny in the morning. Everyone wished they were still asleep.

Teeth first.

As soon as she tried to put the toothpaste on her brush, she dropped the tube and had to lie on the rug to retrieve it from under the sink. Then her toothbrush fell on the floor, too.

Next, into the shower. She was trying to do everything quickly, as she knew Kim would be outside waiting to use the bathroom next. But the water was too hot, then too cold. And she had to jump in and out of the water, covered in soap, trying not to get her hair wet. Failing at that.

This was definitely going to be one of those clumsy days, those days things don't work like they are meant to, those days you get cross at tiny things you shouldn't get cross about, but you do.

The pump on the body wash dispenser was not working in the shower, either. So she lathered herself with her shampoo instead.

The scowl she had dropped on hearing Mahsa in the shower came back. She swore under her breath. Twice. Then a third time, louder, risking being heard. That made her feel a bit better.

And what if she was heard?

Whatever.

Swearing wouldn't make up for the fact that everything was going wrong this morning. And the fact that she was late. And that when things went wrong from the start of the day they carried on going wrong all day.

Did that mean defeat in the semi-final?

Maybe.

Eventually Rocky finished in the bathroom and went back into her bedroom. She dressed in her football tracksuit like she always did on a match day. Trainers on and she was glad not to see anyone else in her flat, nor in the corridor. But there was a queue at the canteen. At least twenty others.

Here we go again, she thought. *More things going wrong.* She checked her watch to see it was ten to eight.

How is it ten to eight?

She hated being late. She hated people being around and in her way and queueing and not being in control of where she could go and when. Rocky looked down the queue and saw that there were no pancakes where they should be. That the first big metal tray of pancakes had gone.

She swore again. This time not silently, as two boys ahead of her looked back and smiled.

Pancakes were her pre-match meal, routine, everything.

So, what could she do? Hope that the second round of pancakes arrived by the time she reached that counter? How long would that take? Pancakes were great on a match day. Carbs. But sweet. With bananas sliced on top and a drizzle of syrup.

She reached the pancake counter. There was just an empty space where the pancake tray should be. This day was rubbish.

Bathroom. Fail.

Seeing housemates. Fail.

On time for breakfast. Fail.

Now pancakes.

Fail. Fail. Fail.

And—deep down—she knew she sounded like a little princess on a match day. Demanding pancakes!

I need pancakes! I'm a footballer and we're

playing in the semi-final today.

Then a hand on her shoulder. She turned. She wanted it to be Kim. With pancakes.

But it wasn't. It was Cody. One of the boys on the school football team. American football. He had his tray loaded already.

"Good luck today," he smiled.

"Thanks." Rocky felt a bit better. Someone being nice to her after last night and all that trouble with her teammates. Then she saw what Cody had on his tray.

Pancakes. Bananas. Syrup. Plus two other plates piled with food.

She stared at them, then at him. She felt like crying.

"You want them?"

Rocky hesitated, but not for long, then nodded.

"I got them for you," Cody laughed. "I saw you were late. I know how you work." He hesitated. "Hmmm. I hope that doesn't sound creepy. I don't mean it to. It's... look, it's a match day. A semi. The biggest soccer day... I mean football day... Mountain Heights have ever had, and we're all behind you."

Several people overhearing the conversations in the queue nodded. A couple whooped.

When Rocky had arrived at Mountain Heights, whooping was one of the things she had hated. It was so American. Now she loved whooping.

She took the plate Cody offered. "Thank you. I owe you."

"Just win today and I'll get you pancakes for a week."

Rocky went to sit outside, away from everyone with her tray of pancakes, juice and coffee.

She stared at the hills as she ate, slowly.

The encounter with Cody had given her a lift. His kindness. His breaking out of his own routine to be nice and to boost someone else. Rocky barely knew Cody. He was usually arm in arm with his boyfriend. Or surrounded by other boys and girls who loved him because he was the captain of the American football team.

But today he had reached out, taken a risk.

The sun was up now, spreading rays of warmth across the football fields. It was already warm enough for a lone eagle to be rising on a thermal over the hills. She watched it, smiling, then she saw a second eagle. They were a pair. Rocky wished Kim was there to see, too. She hoped they'd still be there later.

As Rocky stood to clear her place, she saw Mahsa and Naomi alone at a table across the canteen. Both eating while reading schoolbooks. Rocky grabbed two oranges from the counter and sat down opposite her two friends.

"I won't interrupt long," she said, placing an orange in front of each of the girls. She hoped this gesture would be a bit like Cody's gesture to her. Make them feel like he had made her feel.

It had lifted her.

"Thanks," the two girls said at the same time.

"Listen," Rocky said. "I'm sorry about last night. I'm sorry about being too much. I'm going to do my best to stop myself. I'll do better today. And I can't wait to walk on the pitch with you this afternoon. That's what matters today."

Both Mahsa and Naomi nodded in agreement.

"Us too," Mahsa said.

Naomi smiled. It was a guarded smile, but at least it was a smile.

11

THE MOUNTAIN HEIGHTS team climbed aboard the bus that would take them south to a city called San Clemente. San Clemente was halfway between Los Angeles and San Diego, where the Sundowns were from. A neutral venue for the semi-final had been agreed, meaning that neither team would have a home advantage.

At the beginning of the bus journey, as they pulled out for the drive through the vast city of Los Angeles, Rocky handed out more oranges. One per player. She put them in the hands of each of her teammates with a smile.

"For half time," she said. "Or... well, whenever you need them."

What were they thinking about her? Had they been talking about her being bossy? Or were they not even thinking about her and just had their minds on the game? Rocky had no idea. She hoped it was the latter.

And—also—could they hear the authority draining from her voice?

She had decided that she should make her orange gesture without words. Give each of the players something. Maybe it would work. Maybe it wouldn't. But Cody had made her feel better at breakfast that morning and she wanted to spread the feeling.

Rocky sat with Kim on the coach ride south.

She would have sat with someone else, aware people might think she only ever talked to or sat with Kim, but getting on last, speaking to all the players as they climbed aboard, she found that everyone else seemed to be paired up.

Should she be paranoid about there being no spare seat for her?

No.

She knew it was just a thing. People sat next to who they sat next to. Their best friends. Or the person they always sat with. It was part of their pre-match routine and they would expect Rocky to sit with Kim. It was not a plan to shut her out.

Definitely not.

Stupid thought.

But where did stupid thoughts like that come from?

Was she mad?

Kim was texting when Rocky sat down.

"All good?" Rocky asked, belting up. She always asked. That gave Kim a chance to talk about her mum, but only if she wanted to.

You could just say yes or no to a question like that. If Rocky had said something more direct like How is your mum? then it was harder for Kim to fend off the question.

"Yes," Kim beamed. "That was my mom on the phone. She had a thing this morning. And it's good. Her bloods all suggest the treatment is working. It's great. She's thrilled."

"Brilliant," Rocky said. "You two are so ace. You're so positive. What a time you're going through. I wish I could do more."

Kim stopped Rocky. Hand on her knee.

"What?" Rocky asked. Had she said something insensitive?

"You're doing it again."

"What?"

"Feeling sorry for me."

"But—" Rocky sputtered. She remembered what Kim had said about the difference between their situations to the others last night. A dead parent versus a parent who was ill, but was getting better. "Of course I am," she said. "Your mum has cancer. She's on chemotherapy. It's serious."

"But so are millions of people. And most of them have the treatment and get better. She's not even ill now. The only discomfort she has is from the treatment. She's good. She's planning to take me to Europe for the summer. Travel plans. The future. It's all good."

"But still. I care about you. I want you to know."

"We've talked about this before," Kim interrupted.

Rocky shrugged.

"But you don't buy it," Kim went on.

"I don't."

The bus was out of the side roads now and they were accelerating off a slip road and onto a freeway.

"Can I tell you again?"

"Why?"

"It helps me," Kim smiled.

"Fine. Say it."

"It makes me feel good to say it about me." Kim delivered each sentence clearly and crisply, emphasising each word. "My mom was ill. She is being treated. She is getting better. Much better. I am happy. I am happier than I have ever been because I know how worrying it can be when things go wrong."

"Great," Rocky said.

"And I am lucky to have a friend who cares so much about me that they ask me if I am okay all the time. I feel loved. Thank you."

Rocky didn't know what to say.

Kim nudged her. "Shall we talk about the game? Forget everything else? How you're going to win the ball, then play a perfect through-ball to me and bang…"

*   *   *

AN HOUR INTO the journey, Abby called Rocky forward for a chat. Rocky slipped away, not wanting to wake Kim who was dozing.

Rocky went to sit up at the front of the coach in the seat behind Abby and Jesse, giving them an orange each that she had left in her bag.

"You okay, Rocky?" Abby said.

"Yes, Coach," Rocky replied. "Why? Don't I seem it?"

Make me not captain, Rocky said in her head. But the words didn't make it to her mouth.

"You don't seem yourself. That's all," Abby pressed.

What is myself? Rocky wanted to say. *Not this. You're right. Maybe it's your fault? I wish you'd never made me captain?*

But she didn't.

"I'm fine," she said.

THE BUS JOURNEY took three hours. Then they were in the dressing rooms, Rocky trying to read the vibe in the room. It was tricky. Normally she would be on her feet, chatting to everyone, winding them up so they were all ready to play.

But not today.

Am I letting them down? she asked herself, catching Kim's eye.

It was like she was inside herself.

It was like the whole team was inside itself. Not just her.

Or was it? Maybe it was just her?

Wasn't this the biggest moment in each of their football careers? A state championship semi-final? This might be the best it ever got.

Ever. The thing they exaggerated and told their grandchildren about in sixty years. If they didn't win today.

Maybe they were all nervous?

Maybe this was normal for a semi-final?

And then it struck Rocky.

They were going to lose.

It was a horrible feeling for Rocky. She hated it.

12

A SHRILL WHISTLE. The game started.

And immediately San Diego Sundowns set up just like they had on the video the team had watched back at Mountain Heights. A high line in defence, playing a clever offside trap. Then pressing fiercely the moment Mountain Heights had possession, giving them no time on the ball. Aggressive, too, Rocky thought.

Willing to foul.

She smiled. Well… if they were willing to foul, why not join in? So, with San Diego attacking down the middle, having taken possession off Mahsa at centre-back, Rocky flew to win the ball, taking the ball, then the player.

A clean tackle. As long as you took the ball first, you could send the player flying. The San Diego forward was writhing like she had been shot. But she got no free kick. And no yellow card for Rocky.

A couple of minutes later Rocky challenged for and won the ball. Then she ran with it. She did that knowing what was coming.

She was going to get fouled.

She had seen it on the video. If you hit one of the San Diego players hard—like she had—you got hit back. One touch, two touches, then she was over, her legs taken from behind. Rocky leaped up from the tackle instantly, not a second on the ground, to face her fouler, smiling, bouncing on her feet like a boxer in between rounds.

The San Diego player was yellow carded immediately.

"That all you got?" Rocky asked, grinning, when the referee had turned away. Then she half wished she'd not said it. All this banter and goading weren't what a captain was supposed to do. Captains were leaders, example-makers, not troublemakers.

"No," the taller player grimaced. "I got a lot more."

Rocky closed her eyes, squeezed them shut. *Don't say anything back,* she said to herself. *Just leave it…* But then it came out. She just couldn't help herself.

"Do it again," Rocky said. "Please. Show me what you've got."

The player's eyes flashed wildly and— before she could move towards Rocky—she was quickly pulled away by a teammate.

Rocky had really got to her. Interesting. She

heard herself chuckle. That happy feeling thrumming through her. The buzz of wind up. Not captain-like at all. She had missed that buzz. When she could just do what worked in the moment, without worrying about the team's image or morale.

And now the epiphany.

Like the epiphany the teacher had talked about in the Sylvia Plath poem Rocky had written her report about. That moment when you learn something or realise or understand something about your life. That fire she felt when she went to the opposition player. That buzz of excitement that was like a superpower. She had missed it. It was at that point that Rocky decided she was not going to be a captain for much longer. She had to get away from that. Captaincy killed her game.

The first half of the California State

Championship semi-final was ugly. The crowd of about five hundred was shouting out and booing. There was a negative atmosphere. And Rocky was definitely the target of foul play.

Ten minutes to go until half time, Rocky was fouled for the sixth time. They clearly wanted to kick her off the pitch now. Four players had been yellow carded so far in the match. Three from the opposition. All for fouls on Rocky.

Having had enough, the referee stopped the game and brought the two captains together.

"Girls. A word."

Rocky and her counterpart stood next to the referee. All meek and passive. Behaving how you were meant to with an authority figure.

"This is getting too physical," the referee warned. "We need to play it calmer. If not, there will be red cards and there will be injuries. Do you want that?"

The captain of San Diego said nothing.

"No, Referee," Rocky heard herself say. "We most certainly don't want injuries and red cards. But she does. They do."

There were several players around them now. Mahsa and Naomi, tall, one at each of Rocky's shoulders. Appearing to back her. Rocky liked that.

"Excuse me?" the referee said, face jutting towards Rocky.

The San Diego Sundowns keeper was there too, butting in, causing trouble.

"With respect, Referee," Rocky said, "San Diego Sundowns are the ones playing foul. They are cynical. They play anti-football."

The San Diego keeper thrust her face forward now. "Say what?"

"Anti-football," Rocky said. "It's a term

152

for spoiling the game because you can't play it creatively. The way you play the game is a disgrace."

"And what makes you think you can say how the game is played?" the San Diego captain shot back.

"Because we're better than you."

It was enough. The San Diego captain lunged and punched Rocky on the side of the head. In the melee it was Naomi who took control. She stood between Rocky and her assailant. Towering over other players, she used her arms to keep people apart and her soft voice to calm them.

The San Diego player received a red card.

Rocky, a yellow.

That was worth it, Rocky thought, rubbing her head.

Then Naomi took control.

"We're not thinking," she said, turning

her back on the opposition players, her eyes holding the Mountain Heights team's attention. "We might win this game playing like this. Now we're a player up. But we will not win any more games. We need to use all our energy to play the game, not unplay it. And when we lift that trophy we need to know we have done it the right way. Or what are we?"

Naomi was right, of course. They all knew it. Even the referee.

A calm descended.

At the end of Naomi's short speech, the referee thanked her for helping restore order. Actually called her captain.

Rocky didn't miss that moment.

The scene that had just played out had only made her feel keener to do what had to be done. The referee saw Naomi as a captain; she didn't see Rocky as one. The opposition players were thinking the same. That Naomi was a captain. And Rocky knew she felt the same.

It was clear.

When the whistle went for half time—at nil–nil—Rocky, walking to join her teammates, felt like she was walking on air. The joy that was pulsing through her body from all that delicious wind up came out in a massive grin. She loved altercations like that. They were what she lived for.

Not for being captain. Naomi should be captain.

And Rocky was going to make that happen. Now.

This was it.

She had to do it now, make it happen now.

Jogging over to Abby before their half-time team talk, Rocky stopped next to their coach. This, she knew, wasn't just about this game,

155

this championship. It was about her whole future.

"Coach?"

"Rocky," Abby said, looking worried. Or tired. It was hard to tell. Her voice was even.

"Did you see that?" Rocky said. "Did you see Naomi nail that situation? The ref even called her captain."

"I saw," Abby said, studying Rocky. "I heard."

"Is it possible that you could make her captain?" Rocky asked. "Please?"

"It is something I have been thinking about," Abby admitted, "but let's get through this game first."

"No. No. I actually mean now," Rocky pressed on. "Right now. For the second half. I really think it'd be better for us all. And... I hate it. I hate being captain. When there is someone who would be better at it."

Abby glanced at Jesse, who had joined them, the other players in a huddle a few metres away. Jesse raised his eyebrows at Abby, appearing to concede Rocky had a point.

"I'll speak to Naomi," Abby said.

"I tried, like you said," Rocky went on, not ready to stop. "I really did try it. But I am not good at it. It messes with my head."

A hand on Rocky's shoulder. Abby's eyes were calm. "I get it, Rocky. Now... do you want to come off? Should I sub you?"

Rocky stepped back, her eyes wide. "No. No. I want to be on. The real me. The happy me."

Rocky pulled the captain's armband off her arm and handed it to Abby.

"Thank you," Abby said. Then she handed the armband back.

"What—" Rocky started.

"You go and give it to her," Abby said. "You explain. And Rocky?"

"Coach?"

"Ask her. Don't tell her."

13

Rocky was surprised how quickly Abby agreed to the change of captain. She knew that if she had been injured or sent off, Abby would have made Naomi captain. No question.

And it was clear she was already thinking that way.

Rocky didn't mind that. She was sick of second guessing other people. They think that they did this because I did that or said that. You never really knew.

And what did it matter what other people had in their heads? Guessing what they were thinking was impossible anyway. You were probably wrong half the time. It was what they said, what they did, that mattered.

As her teammates came off the pitch, taking on sports drinks, some lying on the grass to stretch out limbs, Rocky went to Naomi. She held the armband in her hand, making it obvious to Naomi that she had removed it.

"Naomi?"

Rocky saw her glance at the armband, then at her.

"I want to ask you something."

Naomi's face was curious.

"I think I am not the best person to be captain. And we need a captain. And the way you handled that situation at the end there… you were so solid. I want to ask you if you will be captain. Please. Abby has said I can ask you. I think we both know it should have been you all along."

Silence.

Rocky knew others were listening, but that didn't matter. What mattered was her asking Naomi to do something. And making it about Naomi's strengths, not her own weaknesses.

There was a slight smile on Naomi's face. A kind one. Not guarded.

Rocky offered the armband. "Please," she said. "If we're going to win this game—this tournament—we need you as captain. Not me."

Naomi took the armband and rolled it up her arm.

"Thank you. I'll do my best."

Now Rocky exhaled, then smiled.

THE SECOND HALF began. And Rocky was having a wonderful time now she no longer had to bother about motivating her team, thinking about their needs.

She just had to worry about the ball. Who she wanted to have it. Who she didn't want to have it. And how she could make that happen. She did remember from school how she had struggled to focus on too many things at once. Like, six different subjects a day. Six different classrooms. It was difficult.

Maybe she was made for one job. Two at most. Winning the ball before an attack stressed the defence. Controlling the ball and passing to a player who could launch an attack.

It was simple.

And now Rocky did just what she felt she was made for. What she felt she had been born for. Breaking up play. Playing quite deep. Then, once won, delivering the ball to Lexi or Rebecca on either wing. Or Kim or Beth up front. With no time on the ball, because of San Diego pressing the game, she had to live on her instincts.

And it worked.

Throughout the second half, Rocky Race dominated the game. Her team played off her balls entirely. She was a different player. Every opposition attack ended with her as she tackled or blocked or forced an error.

She delivered a masterclass for thirty minutes.

And with Naomi bossing the defence and the whole pitch, things were looking up.

Until they got towards the last fifteen minutes.

Then something changed.

Rocky was used to their opponents running out of steam late in the game. Usually Mountain Heights were fitter, stronger and finished better.

Not today. Today San Diego Sundowns were the fitter team. San Diego's extra pace and stamina was showing. Rocky could see her midfield partners losing out in one-on-ones and her forwards struggling to defend and help out at the back. In addition, San Diego had brought on two speedy subs for the last few minutes.

A fast attack from San Diego led to what became known as The Sacrifice.

Something that would be talked about for days to come, that would spread around Mountain Heights School as one of those stories.

Rocky's sacrifice.

It was another Sundowns attack. The two forward substitutes flew past the Mountain Heights midfield. One with the ball on the right. One without it on the left. And the Mountain Heights defence was all over the place. No structure. Just Rocky and three other defenders scrambling back to try to prevent what looked like a certain goal.

Substitute one fired the ball across to substitute two. Substitute two took two touches then fired the ball past Ella in the Mountain Heights goal.

Time slowed.

And it was clear that Rocky was the only one who could reach it. And it was clear that if she was going to reach it, she would have to push herself.

She ran hard.

Harder than she'd ever run.

Her lungs felt like they would explode. But she would not let the Sundowns take the lead.

She leaped, legs flying, trying to get boot on ball. Anything on ball.

Rocky felt the pain before she hit the goal post. A bolt of lightning tearing up her arm to her shoulder.

You've broken it, she heard the voice in her head.

She swallowed. Face in the grass. On the ground. And, although the pain made her vomit, she looked up to see what the San Diego players were doing.

They were on their knees. Breathing hard. And their faces? They looked… disappointed.

No goal.

Yes!

Rocky had cleared it. She could tell.

"Don't move." It was Jesse.

Pain. Enormous pain.

"Has she broken it?" Kim's voice.

Rocky felt a surge of adrenaline cancelling out the pain. She tried to stand up.

"I'm fine," she said.

The San Diego keeper came over to her now. What was she doing all the way up the pitch?

"Why are you here?" Rocky asked, angry through her pain.

"Penalties," the keeper said.

"What?"

"Full time. Penalties. But you won't be taking one." The keeper was smiling as she whispered. Like she was pleased. Rocky lifted her arm and waved it in the player's face, feeling another surge of pain.

"You've judged it wrong." Rocky stared into the goalkeeper's eyes. "Just like you judged it wrong that I won't be taking a penalty. I will. It looks like all your decisions are wrong today. And that's a shame as you're about to be a goalkeeper in a penalty shoot-out. The one whose teammates will be thinking let them down on the bus on the way back to school."

Rocky knew she had got inside the keeper's head when she saw her opponent's face drop.

14

THE PENALTIES BEGAN with all the players clustered in two groups. San Diego drinking sports drinks. Mountain Heights doing the same, but some eating orange segments. One group had clustered either side of the penalty area, as directed by the referee. Rocky was on her feet, determined not to show how much she was hurting. There was no way she was going to miss taking a penalty.

"Right. I want Kim, Kenzie, Ella, Beth and Rocky to take the first five. In that order."

Naomi.

Rocky was surprised that their new captain

had been so bold. To tell them who was taking the penalties. In any game Rocky had ever played the captain or coach asked for volunteers, so that anyone not in the right mood could back out.

"You are our best five," Naomi went on. "Any questions?"

No one spoke. The rest of the players went to the chosen five and hit them on the back, ruffled their hair. And Rocky smiled. The vibe was good. Naomi had made the vibe good.

Rocky caught the eye of her new captain and nodded gently. She wanted to convey that she was grateful or at least at ease.

Naomi grinned back at her.

This could work, Rocky thought. Then went to stand with her teammates, next to Kim. Watch the action. Carry out the next part of her plan.

"You good?"

"I'm good."

The two friends smiled.

Then Rocky decided to focus on what she could do without the ball. There were nine penalties to be taken before she took hers.

Her plan? To try—subtly—the best she could to psyche out the San Diego keeper. The keeper had been mean to Rocky, saying she hoped she had broken her arm, so she was fair game, wasn't she?

So, Rocky sat, legs crossed, and watched the keeper. And the keeper only. Staring hard. But not aggressively. She could see that the keeper was already glancing over at her. So—when she did—Rocky smiled and waved.

"Dare I ask why you're doing that?" Kim asked, returning from scoring the first penalty and after fist bumping her teammates. The score was 1–1 after one shot each.

"She was glad I'd injured my arm," Rocky said, the pain surging again. Maybe she really had broken it?

"So?" Kim asked.

"So, me and her... we're playing a little game now."

Rocky smiled as Kim looked puzzled. The two friends stood together with their teammates as the next two penalties were saved. Then the subsequent two scored.

2–2 after three penalties each.

Every time a player from either side scored, they were mobbed, and there was cheering from each side. The players from San Diego trying to out-cheer Mountain Heights. And vice versa.

But all the time Rocky stared at the San Diego keeper, pleased she was still looking over, though pretending not to be bothered.

Then San Diego scored with their fourth.

They led 3–2.

Next up was Beth, Kim's striking partner. She stepped up, both sets of players going quiet. Rocky saw that the San Diego keeper had pointed her out to her own captain before she stood between the posts to take her next shot. Rocky felt the eyes of the opposition captain on her. No doubt she was looking for a reason to be cross with Rocky after she'd got her sent off.

Rocky waved, noticing Abby watching her, eyes narrowed.

Beth scored, the San Diego keeper diving the wrong way.

Now Ella walked towards her goal. Followed by a cheer from her Mountain Heights teammates.

The San Diego player stepped up for their last penalty of the initial five and, without any waiting around, hit the ball hard.

It bounced off the post, back to her. The poor girl trapped it skilfully, then dropped to her knees.

She'd missed.

It was 3–3 and Mountain Heights had one penalty left.

Rocky's penalty.

Rocky heard the crowd cheering and saw her teammates congratulating Ella as she came back to stand with them.

And then all eyes were off Ella and on Rocky.

Rocky stood to take the last penalty. She stretched her legs theatrically, eyes on the keeper still. Eyes always on the keeper. Pain building in her arm. She touched the ball twice, then settled it on the penalty spot, still not breaking eye contact with the keeper.

It was time.

Once the referee had blown her whistle

Rocky glanced at one corner of the net. Then the other. She saw the agitated keeper do the same, glancing to her left. Once. Twice. Rocky was in the keeper's head. But—if she missed—the keeper would be in her head. And she didn't want that.

Rocky felt a surge of pain so sharp she almost had to squat to stop herself collapsing. She waited for it to pass, closed her eyes, gritted her teeth, then smashed the ball as hard as she could to the keeper's right.

Goal!

The keeper didn't even move. Mountain Heights had won.

They were in the final of the California State Championship.

Rocky's teammates ran to mob her as soon as the ball hit the back of the net.

Then something happened. She heard a shout, felt a presence next to her, between her and the other girls in white and yellow and blue.

"No, no, no!" It was Naomi's voice. "Back off! Back off! If we need one player fit for the final, we need this one. I am not having my midfield engine sidelined with a broken arm."

Rocky felt an arm around her. Naomi's.

"Come on," her captain said to her, focusing on her and only her as the other players celebrated wildly. "Let's get you looked at properly."

Captaincy. Rocky smiled and allowed the nausea of pain to come at last.

AN HOUR AND a half later, the bus was moving along a highway, fast into the city.

As the coach turned into the driveway of Mountain Heights they heard the driver honk her horn. Then a massive cheer. There were hundreds of students waiting for them. Banners and school flags.

At the end of the turning circle, the American footballers' cheerleaders were doing their thing. And several teachers were there, too. The principal. Dozens of phones held up to take photos.

Kim stared at Rocky. "Oh my God, we're in the final! Can you believe it?"

Rocky grinned and shook her head. She rubbed one of her eyes.

Now the whole team were on their feet, ready to disembark the coach and be celebrated. The whole school was there to welcome them back.

There was a moment of hesitation as the rest of the team—along with Abby and Jesse—waited for Rocky to get off the bus first.

When Rocky realised what was going on, she gestured to Naomi. "Go on. It's all yours," she said. "If you want it?"

"Are you sure?" Naomi said.

"Never more sure about anything," Rocky smiled.

And Naomi walked along the aisle to be the first to emerge from the school bus. As captain.

AFTER THE MUSIC and the dancefloor—Rocky and Kim dancing with Cody and his boyfriend—there were speeches.

The principal saying how proud she was of the girls.

The head of the parents' association congratulating them.

Then Abby. Her voice—for the first time ever—emotional.

"I wanted to speak, just briefly, to you girls directly. I have something to say. Something personal. And it is my way of thanking you. I... I want you to know that this is the third best moment in my soccer career... or football career for some of you."

Rocky heard a cheer and smiled.

"Now, anyone who doesn't know me that well might have missed that I was on the USA teams that won two World Cups."

Another cheer.

"But I did some pretty damn fine things before that. National titles and cups in the US, Japan and Europe. FIFA player of the year. You know. I did good."

More cheering.

"But I am not one to boast about all that. You know that."

Rocky—along with several others—nodded their agreement. This was odd. Why was

Abby bigging herself up? Was she about to announce she was going to be USA coach or something?

"She'd better not be leaving," Kim whispered.

Rocky nodded.

"But it is important for me to know that you understand that reaching the final of the California State Championship as your coach... at a school that has no history of soccer to speak of... is huge for me. I see it as an achievement for me right up there with my best moments in soccer. As a coaching achievement, my finest."

Abby opened her arms.

"And—although I share that achievement with you—the achievement is mostly, wonderfully yours, girls. What you have done as a team. How you have fought back from adversity. How you have trained and shown teamwork, and played so well. You are awesome and I am proud to lead you to that final."

Cheers and chants. Abby raised her hands to calm the noise.

"One last thing."

Silence.

"If we keep that team ethos and if we think and train the best we can, we can be the first team from Mountain Heights to win anything at state level. We can make history. Your children and your children's children, if they come to this school, will see a photograph of you and say 'That was my mom, my grandma.' Just think about that. I did when I won World Cups. I want you to do that now. So… get some rest. This party's over. Let's save our energy for an even bigger party next weekend!"

Huge cheers. That feeling of excitement when you never want a party to end.

Because now Rocky felt happy. The painkillers Jesse had given her were working. Her confused feelings about being captain and her place among her teammates were gone. Evaporated. And she also felt that this was not the erratic sort of happy she sometimes had, the kind that wouldn't last that long because it was just part of her rapid up and downing, the yo-yo of feelings she had felt for months.

This was proper happiness.

She hoped.

Happy like she wanted to stay and be part of this team next year. And be at school here next year. Not go home to England. Not go pro and live a life of football and only football from the age of fifteen.

That she belonged.

And she thought:

How could I have wanted to leave all this?

Would I be happy if I left all this?
Am I… am I… happy?
This was good.

AFTER THE PARTY, Rocky walked back through the school grounds with Kim.

"So, can I say something?" Kim said, watching Mahsa and Naomi go on ahead of them, promising to make hot chocolate for all four of them.

"Sure."

There was something in Kim's tone to suggest that this was serious.

Kim hesitated.

"Go on," Rocky said. "What is it?"

"How do you think your mum would react if you gave up Mountain Heights and went pro?"

Rocky hesitated. It was a big question. Was

it something Kim had been worrying Rocky might do? They were near the end of term. Big decisions were made at times like these.

"She'd ask me lots of questions and she'd help me find the answers to make a decision," Rocky replied at last.

Kim nodded. "Would she think it was a risk?"

"Well, yeah. And it is. But risk is good. If it works out, it works out; if it doesn't, you try something else."

Kim nodded.

"But I don't think I would," Rocky added, thinking she was putting Kim's mind at rest by talking about her own path, her own choices. "I think I'm going to stay at Mountain Heights." Then she added, "As long as you're here."

"What if I got a pro contract?" Kim asked in a quieter voice. "What would you think then?"

Rocky grinned. She loved these fantasies. What if my dream came true? What if your dream came true?

"I'd be thrilled for you. You get a pro contract. With a team in California. Then Team USA come for you. You play in the World Cup final. You win. Your dreams all come true. I want that so much for you. You know exactly what you want. I'd love it."

"Good," Kim said. "That's good."

Part Three:
Final

15

THE HOTEL THAT Mountain Heights had chosen to put their team up in for the California State Championship final in the city of Salinas was sweet, but small.

It was above the beach overlooking the Pacific and called the Nobel Hotel. Rocky had thought they were going to a Novotel, the name of the hotel chain in Europe. But this was nicer than a Novotel. It had only ten rooms. Something that might get called a boutique hotel back in the UK.

The Nobel Hotel didn't have a proper pool, but it did have a water feature that was cool to look at. The kind that spilled over the side without a wall. There were parasols and loungers for the guests to enjoy.

Rocky would have preferred a big pool. She loved a nice swim to relax. Or a game of water volleyball. But that was not to be.

The team had two nights in the hotel. It was a four—sometimes five—hour drive north from LA. Abby had arranged for Rocky and the girls to have one night's rest in the hotel ahead of the game.

"If we were travelling with Team USA, we'd take a night before and one after," Abby said, "so this is what you're getting. The game is not until the evening, so we'll chill the evening before and on the day of the match."

"And what do we do on our morning off?"

"Chill. Sunbathe. It's a shame we don't have a pool. But we have the hotel to ourselves. We want you to relax. This is a reward as much as a preparation."

There was a huge cheer.

"Just stay on the hotel grounds. The next building along is the hotel where Sorrento Stars High School are staying. Look, you can see their pool from here."

Rocky heard Ella complaining. "How come they get a pool?"

"We couldn't stretch to one," Jesse said apologetically.

Rocky frowned. The pool. The lack of a pool. Was that a problem?

THAT EVENING THE Mountain Heights team watched the Sorrento Stars team in their pool. It looked like the whole squad was in it at once. Twenty of them. Rocky noticed that at one point they were playing water volleyball.

Maybe it was a problem.

"That's a big pool," Kim said to Rocky, interrupting her thoughts.

"That's not fair, is it? Just because they have loads of money?"

"They do. They're the richest school in California," Kim said. "My mom said the same company that owns their school owns half the coast here. They're loaded."

That evening, Rocky had expected to see her teammates laughing, stretched out and enjoying the sun with long glasses of one of the several mocktails on the café menu.

But no. There was no sparkle of excitement. Just tension. Everyone was watching the Sorrento Stars squad playing in the swimming pool. You could hear laughter and shrieks coming along the coast. It was annoying. Especially when the whole Sorrento Stars team seemed to stop, then started waving in the direction of Rocky and her teammates before leaping into their pool.

Very annoying.

They'd have to watch all that again tomorrow before the game.

"They know we can see them," Mahsa said.

Kim leaned forward. "They're mocking us."

"They're posting about it online," Kenzie added. "Look."

It was true. The Sorrento team were goading Mountain Heights now.

Rocky felt the tension rise.

This psychological warfare was not good preparation for the big game. She felt a responsibility to fight back. A duty. Wasn't she the wind-up merchant on the Mountain Heights team? Wasn't it her responsibility to act?

Abby and Jesse had been enjoying a coffee

on the patio behind the hotel. Rocky listened in to what they were saying now.

"Watching them play in the pool all day isn't going to do much for morale," Jesse remarked.

Abby nodded. "I know. But what can we do? Empty their pool overnight, so they wake up and find it gone?"

Hearing Jesse's laughter, Rocky gasped at the idea. Then covered her mouth to conceal her smile. She imagined herself creeping down to the pool that night and letting all the water out, then seeing the faces of the Sorrento Stars players the next morning as they emerged with their towels and sunglasses.

But no. Not that. She might even have tried something like that when she was younger. But that was then. She was different now. She knew that. In addition, it would also be good to avoid being arrested the night before the big game.

But something, Rocky said to herself. *We can do something. Something to fill the time tomorrow morning so we don't have to watch them in the pool.*

Rocky glanced at Naomi. She was on her own, staring at the ocean. And Rocky understood that if there was going to be a good idea, it needed to come from their new captain.

"Do you remember when we dyed our hair pink?" Rocky asked.

Naomi's face opened up into a huge grin. "I do. I do. And I was just thinking why don't we..."

Rocky was about to interrupt and say party... we need a party. But she waited. Didn't interrupt.

"Why don't we have a party?" Naomi

suggested. "Like karaoke? Something like that?"

And so they did!

Rocky woke early as she always did the morning of a game. Even if the game was not for hours, the adrenaline was flooding her system.

She grinned when she remembered the night before. All of them in a function room in the hotel. Singing their hearts out, the doors open so that their opponents the next day could hear them having a good time. Abby and Jesse singing a Killers song. A duet that inspired her and Naomi to do a duet, too.

They sang 'We Are Family' by Sister Sledge. Naomi's choice.

A masterstroke.

The song had gone down a storm and ended

with the two of them swaying on the stage together. In front of everyone as they all joined in. To the smiles of Abby.

And now it was the morning after and the song was stuck in Rocky's head.

Rocky needed to calm her mind. An easy run. Before breakfast. That was what she needed. Calm her mind and body down. Pace herself. Although, after the party the night before, she was feeling more relaxed than ever about her place in the Mountain Heights team.

Heading down to the lobby, she saw a familiar figure. Naomi. Staring out at the sea from the hotel patio. She thought she heard her humming the song too.

"Hey," Rocky said. "You okay?"

"Nervous," Naomi replied. "I have no idea what we're going to do all day. Just watch Sorrento Stars in their luxury pool, I suppose. It's not great prep, is it?"

"The girls will be fine. The party. The karaoke. I think we nailed it together. We are family, after all!"

"We are," Naomi laughed. "We could always become a duet if the football goes south."

Rocky laughed too. How good did this feel? She wanted it to last.

"Look… I'm off for an easy run. Round that park," she said. She wanted to get Naomi away from her thoughts. That was not going to help her, or the team. "Want to come?"

Naomi stood. "Yes please. That is just what I need."

So, they ran. Both wearing their Mountain Heights tracksuits. Looking like proper footballers, Rocky thought, they jogged easily round the park, taking in the trees and a stream and then an area of the park where some soccer coaches were setting up goals and cones for drills.

"Kids' training?" Rocky said.

Naomi nodded.

Then one of the coaches called out, "Morning! Morning, girls." Then she stared at the badge on Naomi's tracksuit. "Mountain Heights? You girls are in the state final. Well, good luck."

Rocky and Naomi stopped for a chat. The sun was shining and it felt good to be out and about.

"You coaching?" Rocky asked.

"Sure are," the coach replied.

They talked about coaching, the game, the stadium, the community the coaches worked with. That they did it for free. That this was close to a tough part of town and most parents in the area couldn't afford the fees of soccer schools and often didn't have cars to drive to them anyway.

"Some kids are coming down in an hour.

It'd be great if you stuck around. They'd love to meet some real soccer players."

Rocky glanced at Naomi, who was about to set off running again. She raised her eyebrows and—after a moment—saw a smile creep across Naomi's face.

"Happy to," Naomi said. "Listen, me and Rocky will be back. Yeah, Rocky?"

"Happy to," Rocky echoed her captain.

"We'll have breakfast back at the hotel," Naomi went on, "and I'll bring some other girls down, too. We'd love to help out."

The coach clasped her clipboard to her chest. "That would be… oh yes… that would be so good. Thank you. It will make such a difference to the children. To meet you. To learn from you. See you in a while, yeah?"

Rocky and Naomi jogged back to the hotel where most of the team were having breakfast.

An hour later fifteen players in Mountain Heights tracksuits walked back en masse over the road to the football field to find fifty girls and boys waiting excitedly to be coached.

16

THE STEINBECK SOCCER Stadium—in Salinas—was off the scale. Stands on three sides. Hundreds of fans from both schools waving flags and banners. And others, too. It seemed as if dozens, if not hundreds, of families had turned out to watch the game.

As they walked on the pitch to warm up, Rocky was stunned.

"Have any of you ever played somewhere like this?" she asked. "In front of this many people?"

Lots of heads shaking.

None had.

"Then this is wonderful," Naomi cut in. "A big stadium. A big crowd. A big game. We owe ourselves a big performance."

Then the captain of Mountain Heights School went to bump fists with each of the squad. Rocky smiled because, after the party and after helping the girls train that morning, she was buzzing. They were all buzzing.

"We've got this," she said.

Rocky liked to see that. It was a joy. Now that Naomi was captain she didn't have to worry about being in charge. You could focus on your own game, think your own thoughts, be led, not have to lead. And Rocky had thoughts. The thing that had kept her awake was the rumour that someone had been offered—or was about to be offered—a pro contract at a full-on professional football club in the States.

Who was it who had been offered a place?

Rocky frowned, felt herself being drawn back into her mind. And she didn't want to be there. She wanted to play soccer... or football. It didn't matter. She wanted to be in her body, not her thoughts.

Anyway... there was a game, a big game to be played. How did you focus your mind on that? She half wished her brother was here. The so-called Roy of the Rovers. He could be useful to her now. For once. He knew about big games and finals and about putting your troubles to one side. It had been nice to talk to him a few days before. Very nice.

All through the warm up Rocky heard Naomi praise each of the team.

"Remember the semi-final? How we fought? We fought as a team. We had all sorts going on and we won. In game time and the shout out. We kept our heads.

"We're winners," Naomi went on. "We're

fighters. We might not have been able to afford a hotel with a swimming pool. We might not have a fancy air-conditioned coach. But we have one thing that no other team has. What's that?"

"That we are family," Kim said, without hesitating. And everyone was singing it, laughing.

And that was it. The mood changed. Rocky could feel it. An energy. They were going to win. She knew it. Partly because of the song and partly because of Naomi being captain. She was amazing at it. Rocky would never have thought to say those things. To ask that question. She was even more pleased she didn't have to do that now. Naomi was a better captain, a more fitting leader. And that was fine.

Rocky walked up to Naomi, who was squatting on the pitch, eyes on the grass.

She had done her team talk. She had spoken to every one of her players. Now she was centring herself.

Rocky waited until Naomi stood.

"Naomi?"

"Rocky. Yes. You good?"

"I'm good. Listen… I want you to know that—whatever happens today—I am proud to be playing this final with you and under you. You're the best captain we could have and I wanted you to know that's how I feel."

Naomi nodded. Quiet. Then smiled. "That means a lot. Thank you."

Now they heard again the girl who must be the captain of Sorrento Stars. Lots of shouting. Lots of orders.

"I don't want to see any defenders in their half!" and "Remember there's a five dollar fine if you're caught offside or do a foul throw!"

A different style of leadership. Very different.

Rocky wondered if this was what she had been like when she was captain. She could see that not all the Sorrento players liked being bossed about. They weren't one hundred per cent into their captain, their leader. Rocky recognised those forced smiles. This team was divided. Perhaps they could be broken.

The Sorrento captain went on. "If we do the small things well, we'll get the big things better. And this team? They have no history. They've never been in the semi-final or the quarter-final. They are out of their depth."

It was just a string of clichés, Rocky thought. Then Five dollar fine? Rocky couldn't believe it. And she was saying it so loudly. Making sure Mountain Heights could hear her.

Out of their depth? Really?

This was such a great set up for her to have

a go. It was a gift. A bit of pre-match wind up. The Sorrento captain was giving it out. On purpose so everyone could hear it. Surely, it was only polite to give some back…

"You get a fine for offside or anything," Rocky called across, "I'll pay it. Just go for it, girls."

Several laughs. Even from the opposition players.

Then the Sorrento captain came over, stopping only when she was right in Rocky's face. She placed her hand on Rocky's shoulder. Rocky didn't move. They stood there like two cats about to have a fight.

Now the girl pushed Rocky. It was only a gentle shove. Rocky, seeing it coming, didn't stumble back. She leaned into the push, barely moving.

A howl from the crowd who had spotted there was some pre-match aggro going on.

And the referee was there, eyes on the scene. She was holding a yellow card up to the Sorrento captain. Rocky—who'd never got an opposition player booked before kick off—burst out laughing.

The referee studied Rocky. "Do you want one, too?"

"No thank you, Referee."

"Then shall we get on with this final?"

Rocky knew it was time.

"Yes please," she replied, her eyes fixed on the Sorrento Stars captain.

17

As THEY TOOK up their positions on the pitch the crowd roared. There was chanting. Most of it for Mountain Heights.

Why was that? Rocky wondered. *Why did they have most of the stadium on their side?*

Sorrento Stars High School was closer to Salinas, so it was easier for the fans to get to the stadium. They had a record as a school that won trophies in soccer. Girls and boys. All ages. They had delivered over ten players to the USA teams over the years. And—of course—they were richer. Meaning they could pay for as many students to travel to and watch the game without asking the parents to contribute.

But proximity, history and wealth? Did that mean anything on the day?

It seemed not. The crowd was behind Mountain Heights.

So why?

Then Rocky got it. Understood. When she heard "Naomi—Naomi—Naomi!" being chanted loudly by dozens of children.

Naomi looked confused.

"They're chanting your name," Rocky told her. "It's the kids from the soccer school. They've come to cheer us on."

For a second Naomi looked flummoxed.

"Really?" she asked.

"Really," Rocky grinned.

It was game on.

"We've got this. Come on, girls." Rocky heard Naomi being captain. A good captain.

She'd timed what she had said perfectly.

And then, above the chants and cheers, Rocky heard a voice.

"Come on, Rocky!"

Weird. Now it was Rocky's turn to look flummoxed.

She looked round.

The voice had come from high up in the stands. Rocky had to shield her eyes to look. But she saw nothing. And yet her heart was hammering, because of the voice. That voice.

It sounded like Dad.

Rocky smiled. The idea that Dad was alive and here. Or even not alive, but here as a ghost or something like that. It was a nice idea. Not an upsetting idea. She would let it go for now. Think about it later. But maybe— just maybe—allowing herself to think happy memories about him made her hearing his voice possible.

The whistle for the kick off went. And immediately Rocky became focused. Everything else was off the pitch.

The game was different. Shockingly different.

Sometimes you come up against a team that is good. Really good. Clearly better than you. And—even though you are playing at your best—they are just on another level.

Today was the day.

You have to accept that. It happens.

And the truth was that Rocky and Mountain Heights were playing well. They were tight at the back. The structure was right. Rocky felt she was winning the ball and playing it forward.

But Sorrento Stars were just… just better. And the annoying thing was that their captain—the one Rocky had had the run in with—was bossing it in midfield. After fifteen minutes she had already won the ball from

Rocky three times. Firm tackles, winning the ball first, then leaving a leg to hurt Rocky.

She was tough.

She was brutal.

But she was accurate. Playing within the rules of the game, right under the referee's nose.

And Rocky had to admire her style. She was playing on a yellow card, too. One more booking and she was off and the game was changed substantially, but she still confidently went about her way.

Goal one came after seventeen minutes.

The ball won in the space between Rocky and her forwards. A pass wide. The Sorrento Stars winger tearing Rachel, then Rebecca, to ribbons down the left. A crisp cross and—with three players attacking the header, lined up as if to score, like a video game gone crazy—a bullet header.

0-1.

The second goal was a long ball.

After half an hour of controlled tight passing at speed, the ball was rolled back to the Sorrento Stars keeper and she hoofed it so it landed five metres short of the Mountain Heights penalty area.

One bounce. A touch by one of the Sorrento Stars wingers, a flick, then a volley past Ella in the Mountain Heights net.

0-2.

This was bad. Rocky knew it was bad.

Was it over?

Rocky was reminded of going to watch Melchester Rovers and seeing them overrun by another team. One of those games where you fear the team you are watching are going to score every time they attack.

It felt horrible watching. But worse on the pitch being part of it.

As the ball was retrieved for the restart, Rocky looked to her captain. Was Naomi okay?

Yes, she was. Of course she was.

Because Naomi was doing everything right. Calling out to players. Encouraging them.

"Ten minutes to half time," Naomi shouted. "Let's get one back before the break. If we go in at two–one it's a completely different game."

Rocky nodded. "That's right. Come on, girls."

Then Naomi was in her face. "And you most of all. You're ball-watching, Rocky. I've never seen you so passive. It's like you're in the stands watching. You might be watching in the stands in the second half if you don't get your stuff together."

Rocky put her hands to her forehead.

What was this? Ball-watching? And Rocky

knew it was true. She had been watching, even admiring, what the opposition were doing. Naomi was having a go at her for doing exactly what Rocky had had a go at her for doing in the quarter-final. And she was right. And—on top of that—she had the authority to say so. She was captain, wasn't she?

Rocky nodded. "You're right. I'm sorry."

"You need to win every ball off this girl," Naomi ordered. "I thought you were supposed to be in her head. But you're not. She's in yours. She's out-Rockying you."

Rocky could have laughed at Naomi's brutal takedown.

Her captain had nailed it.

Utterly.

Having watched Naomi go and speak one to one with several of her other teammates, Rocky felt galvanised.

"Come on!" she shouted as loud as she could, as they got ready to restart the game for the second time. "Do what Naomi says. Fight for this!"

There was something about being reminded what she was good at and what she needed to do that fired Rocky up.

She felt free.

Free because she had been told what to do, instead of reacting to the voices in her head telling her she was good at this and bad at that. Or it would be better to do this than that.

The freedom to not be controlled by her own mind was amazing.

She was part of a machine.

All she needed were simple instructions that came from outside her head.

And she was getting them from Naomi.

Now she would win every ball. Because that is what she had been asked to do.

Dominate the midfield. Win the ball. Or at least break up opposition play. Then get the ball to a forward.

Simple. Like Naomi had said.

It was game-changing.

And, having seen Naomi speak to her other teammates and seeing their improvement, Rocky knew the change in the game was coming from their captain's one-to-ones.

It was amazing.

Rocky won tackle after tackle now. Sometimes she half fouled players on the opposition team. She heard the referee shout a warning to her more than once.

But the Sorrento Stars players were backing off. Their control of the midfield was gone. And, therefore, the game was utterly different.

This was good. The Sorrento Stars players could see Rocky was more motivated and they feared her.

Except the captain. The blonde ponytailed soccer star was still going at it one hundred per cent.

And, because of that, the last five minutes of the first half were eventful.

Very eventful.

The first incident was Rocky going in on the opposition captain and catching her boot-before-ball. She'd not gone in to injure the player, hurt her, but it had been a fierce tackle. The girl went down, but interestingly she didn't make a meal of it and roll around like she'd been shot. She just got onto her hands and knees and—wanting to avoid a booking—Rocky took her hand and helped her up.

Rocky still received a yellow card. And a smile from her opposite number. And a nice smile. Even though the Sorrento Stars supporters were booing Rocky for foul play.

The second incident before half time was a result of Rocky taking a pass off Mahsa, dodging two not very convincing tackle attempts, playing a rapid pass up to Beth, who then, with a deft flick, played Kim in.

There was a gasp from the crowd. Kim was there. The defence sliced open by Rocky, then Rebecca.

One on one with the Sorrento Stars keeper, Rocky's best friend lofted the ball over the keeper as she scrambled out of her goal to narrow the angles.

Goal. A beauty.

1–2.

And now the energy changed! It was like the pitch had been tipped on its axis and everything was suddenly rolling Mountain Heights' way. They had wounded the opposition. They had got the goal that Naomi had demanded by half time. Going in at one down was so much better than being two to nothing. Like their captain had said.

The third incident was—for Rocky—the most interesting.

There were seconds on the clock before half time. Some of the crowd were already heading to the toilets and the coffee bar.

In a replica of the move that had brought the goal, Rocky took a pass from Mahsa and saw Kenzie move into space, and Kim, tight against the Sorrento Stars defence.

She took the ball, then, with a clever turn, dodged her marker and was set to pass the ball to Beth. Then she felt the Sorrento Stars captain slide in and take both her and the ball.

Rocky was on the ground. Her leg hurt. It wasn't a great tackle. Easily a booking for her fouler if Rocky did anything but jump back up. And therefore a red card.

And yet that is what she did.

Rocky found herself instantly on her feet. Even though the Mountain Heights fans were booing Rocky's assailant, she leaped up and touched hands with her.

A sporting gesture. A gesture that showed that both players respected each other and their clashes were just part of the game.

Rocky watched the referee's hand hesitate over her front pocket, then move away, then blow the whistle for half time. Then Rocky looked up into the crowd. The Mountain Heights fans. They had sat back down. Except for two figures.

A woman with short blonde hair in a bob style. And a tall, fit-looking lad with a flash of blond hair the same colour as the woman's. Rocky studied them closely. Or as closely as she could from a hundred metres.

It couldn't be.

Was it them?

They were home in England. They'd have said if they were coming over!

Or would they?

No, it wasn't. It was just wishful thinking.

"Rocky? You okay? You concussed?"

It was Naomi's voice. She was close now. "That foul," Rocky's captain asked, "did it hurt you?"

Rocky shook her head. "No. I'm sorry, I was distracted." Rocky looked at the huddle forming. It was half time. She'd not even heard the whistle. Her teammates were drinking sports drinks, eating orange segments.

She wanted some of that. She glanced into the fans again, but saw no one. She'd imagined her family there to watch. That was all.

The oranges, yes. Back to the oranges. But more the team bonding, the electricity and power she felt when they were all connected. The thought of an electricity circuit. The kind of thing they'd been studying in Science. Then she went to join in. To add power to the circuit. To do what she could to help Abby and Naomi, to help any of her teammates. Because she knew they had a chance.

Of winning.

18

As the teams took their positions for the second half amid lots of shouting on the pitch and from the stands, Rocky noticed two women placing a golden trophy on a table at the foot of one of the stands.

She didn't want to see that yet. It was too soon, too distracting.

So Rocky cast her eyes up into the crowd, scanning for faces, trying to find the couple she had seen. First she saw Kim's mum, and a woman in posh clothes who looked out of place, talking to her, handing her something. What was that? And then her mind was torn away from that scenario to two very familiar figures.

Her mother.

Her brother.

Both waving, smiling. Roy had a Mountain Heights flag round him like a cape, two girls leaning into him, grinning, taking selfies.

They probably knew he was a Premier League footballer.

Yes, it was clear they did.

Rocky waved back, controlling a surge of emotion, then turned to look at the ball, then Naomi.

"Will you stop looking at that boy in the stands?" Naomi said. "As your captain I really think you should have your eyes on the game."

"He is the last person in the world I would be looking at like that, thank you very much," Rocky laughed. "He's my brother!"

"What, like Roy Race, the footballer?" asked one of the opposition players, listening in. "I thought I'd seen him. He's the one who does that Rocket volley move?"

Rocky rolled her eyes. Why did her brother always steal the show when he arrived anywhere? The famous footballer. His famous Rocket. Even here on her big day?

"Forty-five minutes," Naomi shouted, mind back on the game. "A hundred percent. You know what each of you have to do. I want you to visualise it. See it."

Rocky felt that rush of power again from being part of this team. From being coached by Abby. From being captained by Naomi. She spent a moment doing what Naomi had suggested. Visualise celebrating at the end. Visualise seeing Naomi lift that trophy. Visualise a medal being placed round her neck and a photograph of the team in the school foyer looking older and older as the years went by, celebrating the first team of any sport, girls or boys, who lifted a California State Championship title.

It was going to happen.

History. They could make history.

Rocky believed it.

She believed it so much that she knew that she would never get over the disappointment if they failed. She would carry either the glory or the sadness with her for the rest of her life.

But that was fine.

To achieve that glory she was willing to take the gamble. Better to have loved and lost than never to have loved at all, she thought.

The second half began.

Tackle after tackle flew in. Passes went astray. Players went down.

It was fierce.

As the game wore on, Rocky could feel the energy draining from her legs and body—and she could see the same in all the other players—but she had to keep going.

Still 2–1 down with forty minutes left. Thirty minutes. Twenty.

It couldn't end like this.

In defeat.

It must not.

Then somehow Rocky found herself on the wing. Seeing Kenzie filling into her place on the field, she took the ball and ran with it. There were tired bodies around her and she pushed on, hearing the roar of the crowd, using it to fill her body with energy she didn't know she had.

Tight along the touchline, then she worked her way in, skipping over two tackles, the captain of Sorrento Stars pulling at her shirt, then releasing a pass that skimmed across the grass to Beth, who, drawing both remaining defenders, dummied, and there was Kim, pirouetting like a ballerina, side-footing the ball past the dive of the Sorrento Stars keeper and the net billowing.

Goal!

They had it.

2–2.

Two goals each with ten minutes to go.

"Come on!" It was Naomi's voice. "We win this! And we win it now! Keep focus. We need a winner."

Over her captain's voice, Rocky heard the Sorrento Stars captain calling out to her players, too.

Ten minutes to avoid a penalty shoot-out. Ten minutes to win a state championship.

Rocky wanted so much to push up the pace of the game, fill it with energy. If they just gave it everything. For ten minutes. Six hundred seconds. That was all.

But there was fear in the game now. The dynamic had changed. Before it had been one team desperately trying to equalise, the other team equally desperately trying to hold their lead. The desire to make something happen, to affect the game in a positive way.

But now? That fear of making the mistake that left you and your teammates and your school the losers.

Rocky could feel it.

Pass, pass, pass.

Then players going down, needing medics.

The game was slowing. It was dying.

It was the kind of game that each team would get one more chance to score in. When one team missed their chance and watched the other team go down the other end and score.

It was like it was written down in a book.

Mountain Heights were the first team to have that last chance.

Three minutes on the clock.

Rocky wanted to make something happen amid all the careful football. She took the ball up in her own half, then went for it. A marauding run, direct on goal, slaloming two tackles, then a third that was an attempted foul. A red card if they'd made contact.

Now Rocky was approaching the edge of the Sorrento Stars penalty area, and she drew her foot back to shoot.

Then a tackle.

Perfect, the ball knocked from under her as she drew her leg back to shoot.

Rocky watched as the ball spun wide towards the touchline, as she tried to regain her balance, several attackers and defenders ahead of her now. A mad scramble into the box, because now, somehow, Naomi, who had been behind Rocky moments ago, was on the wing, cutting in, then firing in a cross that hit the first defender then ballooned back out to Rocky.

In space.

Eighteen metres out.

A penalty area packed with players. Some down. Others alert, moving to close her down.

And, with no time to allow the ball to drop, to control it, Rocky hit it on the volley.

19

THE WORLD SEEMED to stop the moment Rocky's foot connected with the ball.

Do you know the feeling? That timelessness. The times in your life when something amazing or terrifying happens to you and time slows down, giving you the space to see and hear and feel the world and to think thoughts you might never think in normal time.

It's weird and it's hard to put into words. But it happens. And it was happening now. To Rocky Race.

As her boot made contact with the ball, Rocky channelled all the power and control in her body to hit it hard, but keep it down and on target. She was using all the techniques she had been taught by her coaches, by her brother and Ffion, as well as the experience of hundreds of hours just practising, her whole life in football distilled into this one minute.

As the ball left her foot—and still feeling as if she was watching her life in slow motion—she saw the faces of two of the Sorrento Stars defenders, both up close to her, their eyes moving from Rocky to the ball and where the ball was going, as one tried to pull her down by her shirt.

Then time slowed even more.

For a moment.

And Rocky knew—in this extra time she was given—that she did not want to go home to Melchester and live with Mum and maybe play lower league football in England with the half chance of making it in the Women's Super League; that she did not want to go professional in the USA at the age of sixteen and devote her life entirely to high pressure US soccer until she succeeded or failed and was left with nothing.

Not that.

Not yet anyway.

What Rocky wanted to do was be on this team. To be with Kim and Naomi and Mahsa. And the others. To grow with them. To build on the achievement that this whole year, ending with this goal, meant. And the school work, too. She wanted that. And to live in California. Be visited by her mum. The light, the hills, the ocean. This was her life now. She had found a life worth living.

We are family. That song again.

The epiphany astonished her. It was so obvious that was the path she should take.

And now time was racing forwards again. The ball smashing against the cross bar, then Rocky being pulled down by the shorts and the sound of a massive cheer from the stands.

It was in. She knew it was in. Rocky had scored.

She rolled onto her back and looked into the crowd.

To be eye to eye with her mum.

How amazing was that? She could look into a crowd of a thousand people and lock onto her mum's face and see her smile. And see—also—a happy woman. How Rocky loved to make her mum happy.

Next to her, Roy was leaping around celebrating. But Mum was just looking at her, grinning.

Then Naomi was there, holding back the entire Mountain Heights team who wanted to jump on Rocky.

"Back! Back, everyone!" Naomi shouted above the celebrations. "Are you hurt?"

Rocky shook her head and grasped the hand that was put out for her to take, thinking it was Naomi's. But it wasn't. The hand lifted her up and she saw it belonged to the Sorrento Stars captain.

"Great goal," the girl said. "But this isn't over yet."

It was 3–2 to Mountain Heights. Ten minutes to go. The Sorrento Stars captain was right: it wasn't over.

Ten minutes from being crowned state champions. Ten minutes was a long time in football if you wanted to hold onto a lead.

The last phase of the game was furious and fast. It was back to the frenzy of a game that needed winning or saving. No more fear of penalties. No worries about making a mistake. A proper game. And both sets of fans were screaming and shouting with increasing desperation.

And it could have seemed like chaos.

But it wasn't.

All Rocky could hear was the calm and clear—if loud—voice of her captain. Naomi, shaping the team with her voice.

The game needed that. Mountain Heights needed that.

And then it was all but over. As Mountain Heights broke with their next attack after the goal, Rocky watched the last defender take Kim's legs from behind.

Without hesitating, the referee thrust a red card at the defender.

It was a cynical tackle. A clear red card. But someone wasn't happy about it.

The Sorrento Stars captain pushed the referee to object. It was like one of those short films you see on social media. A moment of madness that you watch over and over on a loop. The referee on the ground. The Sorrento Stars captain stooping down to help her back to her feet, and then she was off, too.

Two red cards. Sorrento Stars had no chance now. Did they?

Standing next to Kim, both shattered and relieved to have a break from the frenzy, Rocky watched the Sorrento Stars captain leave the pitch, making a detour to come straight past Rocky and Kim.

Rocky was pleased. She wanted to see the girl's face. Would she be snarling? Would she be sobbing? Would she lash out again? Was she about to start a fight?

Rocky was ready for anything, then found herself stepping forward to protect Kim.

The girl stopped in front of her.

"By the way, I'm Carly," she said. She put her hand out, and when Rocky took it to shake,

Carly held onto it for a moment longer than necessary. "I was wondering if you'd like to come on a date with me. After all this."

And then the Sorrento Stars captain was gone. Walking off the pitch. Her head down.

Rocky was stunned by the question. She'd been asked out before. Not many times. But only by boys. Until now.

"Focus!" she heard Naomi shout at her. "Rocky, get on it."

Rocky closed her eyes for a second and did what her captain asked, putting all other things out of her mind.

The last minutes of the game petered out after the sendings-off. Down to nine players, Sorrento Stars had nothing left, really. And, when the whistle blew for full time, their players fell to the ground, heads in hands.

The Mountain Heights girls roared and danced and grinned wildly.

After a few moments, Rocky went to shake the hands of some of the opposition, still confused by what their captain had asked her, then she went back to join her teammates with Abby and Jesse, surrounded by fans. A hug with Kim that became a huddle with the team that became a mob of other students from Mountain Heights.

What a moment!

They were the California State Champions!

Extracting herself from the melee again, seeing Kim and her mum embracing, then talking to the well-dressed woman, confused by the intensity of it all now, even overwhelmed by it, Rocky stepped away from her teammates and looked up into the stand to see Mum and Roy on their feet. Both clapping and grinning, then waving when they saw her looking.

And something came back to Rocky.

When she was a kid, she was watching the Wimbledon tennis final on TV with her mum, and one of the players had climbed up the stand, through the seats to hug his mum or girlfriend, someone he loved, someone he was happy to see.

Rocky remembered how her mum had adored it. Had thought it was the most lovely thing she'd seen.

Rocky wanted to do that for her mum. Make her feel loved like that.

And she found herself running. Through the edge of the crowd. Then up towards the aisle to her mother's row. Hands clapping her on the back. Shouts, questions, chaos.

"Excuse me... sorry... I need to get to..." Rocky heard herself saying. She could feel the eyes of hundreds on her. Of heads turning to watch her. But she didn't care. She only had eyes for her mum.

Reaching her mum, having not seen her or hugged her in weeks, thousands of miles between them, Rocky threw her arms round her.

"Brilliant, love. Brilliant." Mum was sobbing.

Rocky looked over Mum's shoulder and saw her brother.

"Well done. I'm proud of you."

"Thanks, Roy," Rocky gasped, as Mum squeezed her so hard she felt she might burst.

After the hugs and the tears, Rocky walked Roy and Mum down to meet her friends and teammates, for the trophy and medals.

Down the steps. More hugs and cheers and a Mountain Heights flag draped around her by Cody and his boyfriend.

As they reached the pitch, Rocky's brother turned to her.

"And, by the way," he said. "You're welcome."

"What?" Rocky asked.

"You're welcome."

"For what?"

"For the idea. For that goal you scored. On the volley. Off the bar. Full power. They call it the Rocket. Roy's Rocket. I'll let you have that one. For free."

"I think you'll find," Rocky said to him, "that times have changed, Roy. It's known as Rocky's Rocket now. Sounds better, doesn't it?"

THERE WAS ANOTHER party that night. Hundreds of children packing the sports fields to welcome home the California State Champions—Mountain Heights School of LA.

With their trophy!

Abby gave a speech.

The principal gave a speech.

Then Naomi spoke. A short address about her teammates and coaches and how this school—this country—had given her experiences and dreams she never imagined she could have, even a year ago.

Her last words were not about football or school work.

"The biggest thing I've taken from this," Naomi said, "is that the best lessons are not learned on the training field or in the classroom, but that they are made through friendships. And that—in some ways—those lessons are the hardest to understand. But I think I have come to understand. So, my last thank you is to Mahsa, to Kim and to Rocky. For their friendship."

A huge cheer.

20

KIM ASKED ROCKY to walk with her on the football fields. One last lap before the end of the summer term.

"That girl who asked you out?" she said. "What are you going to do?"

"She's messaged me," Rocky said. "She must have found me on social media. I've not replied."

"Okay," Kim said.

A pause.

"Listen," Kim said.

Rocky stopped and looked at her friend. There was something in her tone of voice. An edge. Whatever she wanted Rocky to listen to, it was important.

"What's up, Kim?"

Was it the girl asking her out? Was that a problem for Kim? And—if so—what did that mean?

Or was it her mum? Was her mum ill again? Was the cancer back?

Kim smiled. "It's not Mom," she said, reading Rocky's concerned face. "But it's big."

"Okay?"

"I've… I've been offered a deal to go pro. In New York."

Rocky's mind was spiralling. And then she remembered. The woman in the suit. At the final. Talking to Kim's mum. She was from a football club. Of course!

"That is awesome," Rocky said. She was excited for her friend. Her friend whose dream had come true.

Then her mind began to explore what this great news for Kim meant to her, Rocky. What did it mean? Rocky's whole future suddenly looked different.

"You'll take it?" Rocky plastered on a smile, worried her face might be giving away her misgivings.

"I have to," Kim said gently.

"You'd better," Rocky said firmly.

Their eyes met. There were no words between them now.

"I'm sorry," Kim said.

"For what?"

"That I won't be here with you. For you."

Rocky put both hands on Kim's shoulders.

"We," Rocky said, "will be friends for life, wherever we live. We will always be with each other and there for each other."

Kim smiled. "Yes," she said.

"Until we meet in the World Cup final,"

Rocky grinned. "Then, for ninety minutes, it's war."

Acknowledgments

I have really enjoyed working on *Soccer Diaries 3*. Amy Borsuk and Chiara Mestieri have been brilliant editors, helping me get the best out of Rocky Race and keeping it fun for Rocky and for me. Thanks, too, to Jamie Elby for his hard work helping Rocky find readers. And to Tamsin Shelton for an excellent copy edit. As with all the Rocky and Roy books, my thanks to Simon Robinson, who gave me a tough team talk after reading the first draft of this book. Necessarily.

About the Author

Tom Palmer is a best-selling children's author from Leeds, England. He has written dozens of books for children, including the *Football Academy* series, and continues to inspire young readers up and down the UK. He supports Leeds United.

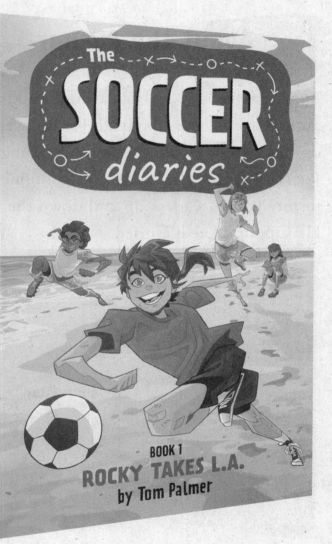

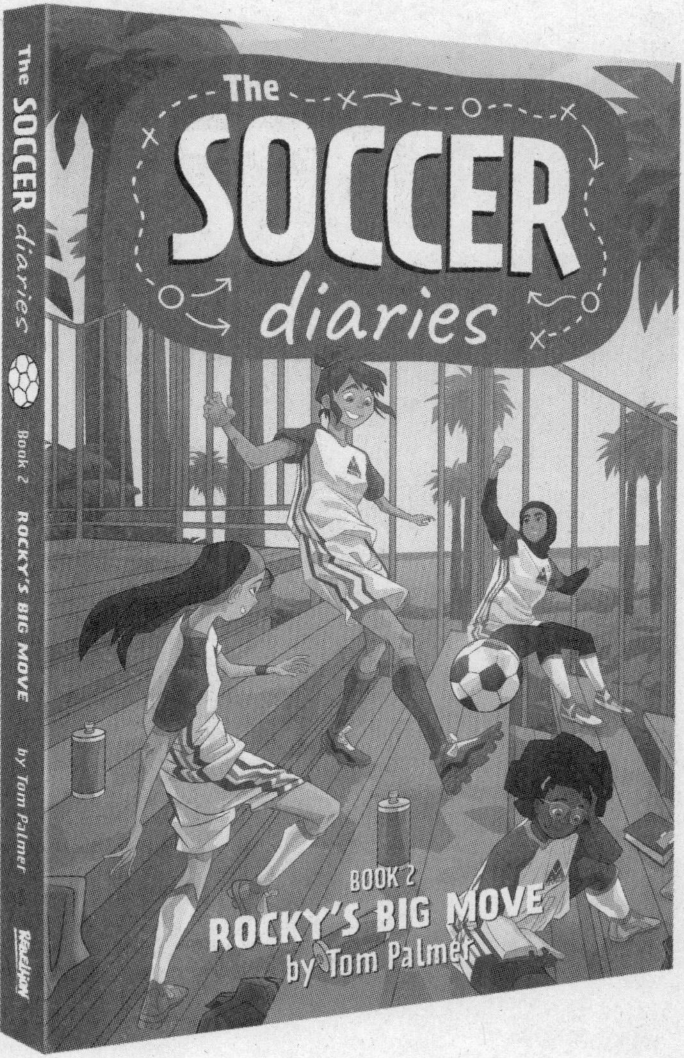
The SOCCER diaries
Book 2 ROCKY'S BIG MOVE
by Tom Palmer
The SOCCER diaries
BOOK 2
ROCKY'S BIG MOVE
by Tom Palmer

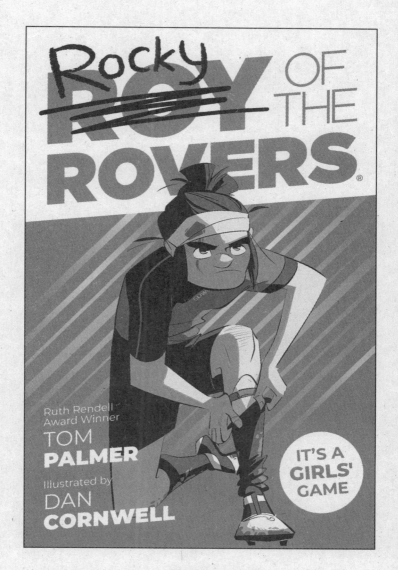